MICKEY RORY

Beyond the North Tower

This book was professionally typeset on Reedsy.
Find out more at reedsy.com

This is dedicated to the two young ladies whose enjoyment of the original oral presentation of Roisin's story inspired this book and to my family for their patience while I wrote and rewrote.
Mickey

Contents

1

I. Tragedy

The rider was brisk and assured. He rode swiftly down the narrow trail that edged the cliff overlooking the sea. There was a recklessness about him that angered the colonel. As he brushed past, the colonel could see the ruthless arrogance of aristocracy in the young rider's eyes. He registered the emblem on the clasp of the cloak, a great cat springing, its forelegs outstretched, claws bared, its teeth white against the tawny background.

"Out of my way," came the soft snarl of voice from close behind him and he heard a horse nicker and his niece gasp.

The scream that followed was a remorseless icy blade that ripped through the colonel's senses tearing apart his past and present lives forever. In an instant, it brought his mind to full attention. He wheeled his horse to view a scene that near tore his heart from his chest. A dappled mare, eyes wide, scrabbling desperately for hold, two legs already beyond the crumbling mountain pathway and over the abyss. Her young rider with a shrill, panicked cry pressed closely to her, arms wrapped tightly about her neck. It was an unforgettable image etching itself in the deepest regions of the colonel's brain, burned in place for the remainder of his life.

He leaped from the saddle, arms outstretched to grasp the young rider and pull her from danger. At the extent of his reach, he frantically grasped for her nearest hand that was clasped in a vice grip of fear on the mare's neck. The colonel still stretching tried desperately to hold it and pull it loose. Too late!

With a final scream, the mare slipped over the edge. The child astride it, shifted towards him, arms breaking loose from their grip on the horse's neck and grabbing desperately at the outstretched fingers of the colonel's hand. There was a fleeting moment of contact, then, nothing. For what seemed like a helpless forever, the colonel and his young niece's eyes met, then she was gone. There was no mare, no child, no screams, just the far-off pounding of the surf and the startled cry of a seabird, its quiet flight along the cliff side interrupted.

A last frantic dive to reach the small hand as it dropped away had left the colonel lying face down against the broken earth that edged the trail. Slowly he pulled himself closer to look down. Between the folded stone of the cliff face and the unbroken stretch of silver blue sea, there was, far below, a tiny stretch of cockleshell strand. On that strand, horse and rider, now separated, were two still, small figures.

The rider might have been gone from sight as the colonel raised himself from the edge of the cliff, but he would never forget the crest or the look of cold arrogance on the fine features of the face.

With a burst of reflex honed sharp from years in His Majesty's service, the colonel pushed himself to his feet, raced to his steed and leaped to its saddle. Within seconds, the two were hurtling at breakneck speed down the trail that ran along the cliff's edge overlooking the sea.

Where the decline became less steep, horse and rider veered from the path to slip and slide their way to where the sea met the land. Then back along the water's edge, they raced. Across cockleshell and sand and through shallows where the water lapped as high as the stallion's breast they pressed on until they reached the tiny strand where horse and rider lay.

The colonel dismounted and raced towards the twisted figure of the young girl. Without so much as a sidelong glance, he passed the mare, which was writhing and groaning and trying desperately to rise up on its shattered legs. Falling to his knees beside the child, he bent over her, brushing a honey blond tress from her face. He studied her face, gently touching a droplet of blood that lay at the corner of her mouth. He trembled as he closed the lids over her sightless, fading eyes.

Although no stranger to death, the colonel could not prevent the tears that filled his eyes and shook his body. With a gentle touch, he picked up his niece, as light as a cloud in his arms, carried her to his horse, laid her across the saddle and secured her. His hand brushed against the coolness of her cheek as he pulled the steel blue, pearl-handled revolver from the holster attached to his military saddle. With a quick check of the chamber, he walked back to where the mare continued to writhe and whinny in her pain.

Through tear clouded and burning eyes he surveyed her body, then bent down beside her, resting his hand against her muzzle. She stopped her agonized movement and gazed up at him with large brown eyes. He patted her muzzle as he set the barrel of his revolver just behind her ear and pulled the trigger. The nearness of flesh muffled the pistol's report. The mare made one sharp arching motion and then lay still.

Three days later, the same Colonel stood before his king. This time his outstretched hands held across them a field officer's Sabre, a weapon both practical and ceremonial, along with the links of rank as he bent to lay them at the foot of the throne. He looked straight ahead to avoid seeing the young boy who shook with tears in his mother's comforting embrace.

The king fidgeted with discomfort on his formal throne and looked down at his hands as if examining them for the first time. Then, looking up, he met the colonel's eyes squarely. "So, there is no way we can change your mind," said the king in tones that were neither statement nor question.

"No, your highness, there isn't." replied the colonel with conviction.

"You'll be sorely missed," said the king, turning to look at the tearful boy at his side. "It will be a great loss to us all."

"To me as well, majesty. My years of service to you and to Prince Rafael and to all your family are ones I will cherish. But, I must leave. I can no longer serve as a member of the Life Guard. Riding at my niece's side I could not save her how could I continue to accept such responsibility for my liege and heir to the crown of this nation I have served for so many years."?

"It is a tragic thing, your niece," said the king, "but it was an accident. You could not have anticipated…"

"Not justifiable when one dedicates his whole life to anticipating and preventing anything that might risk the wellbeing of one's charge, highness." There was a finality to the colonel's tone."

"Very well, then, Colonel," said the king, "I accept your resignation as a member of the Royal Life Guards and accept your sword, but only to hold them for you. I neither rescind the ranking you have gained with honor, nor your rights as an officer of the crown."

"An unnecessary kindness Your Majesty...."

"Enough, enough..., go, do what you have to. I understand." The king's tone softened. "You know you will always be welcome here, Arram. Our kingdom, our home is always open to you." He stopped.

The colonel bowed, setting the sword at the king's feet. He turned to smile at the crown prince and his mother, both of whom returned his smile through tears. He then turned and walked from the room. He didn't see the Prince run to hug his father, or the two following him with their eyes until the huge doors clanged shut behind him. As he passed he did see among the crowd of courtiers lining his path the emblem of the great cat springing, against the tawny background below a pair of icy, arrogant eyes.

Colonel Arram Nevil, the youngest man to ever hold that rank in the Imperial Life Guards, Personal bodyguard to Raphael crown prince, loyal soldier, faithful servant, passed through the palace gates to the salutes of his fellows. He disappeared into the crowds of people that carried on their lives around the palace and its enormous towers.

His search for personal peace led him down pathways to places he had never suspected even existed. Life among the common folk was a rude one for the schooled and aristocratic former Royal Life Guard, yet he slipped into the role of a rough-spoken peasant with untold ease

He returned years later to settle in a small house on the outskirts of the capital. He had learned many things on his travels and was able to make a meager living selling arcane and amusing creations of his own construction in one of the lesser markets of the city. His days with the palace guard were far behind him. However, and unbeknownst to him, they were not yet finished.

II. Newly Minted GuardII. Newly Minted Guard

"Company…. halt!"

The crisp snap of the Sergeant's command cut through the skirl of pipes and the rattle of drums. In unison, fifty steel soled boots slammed down against the cobblestones as the last note from the pipes hung on the air then faded away leaving only the muted tapping of the drums to break the silence.

Standing rigidly at attention, Underlieutenant Matricht 's gaze wandered past the Sergeant towards the Royal Palace which stood in imposing majesty just beyond the ornate filigree of the main gates. For Matricht, this moment was the realization of a life-long dream. As long as he could remember, he had wanted to be an officer of the Imperial Life Guards.

If he had forgotten why he had the dream, his mother had reminded him again that morning, as she had many times throughout his life. "My goodness," she said, reaching out to smooth his cheek just before muster. "You look so handsome in your uniform, just like your uncle did so many years ago."

and a look of sadness would darken her face.

"I wish he was here to see this day. I'm sure he would be as proud as we all are." and she put her arm around the shoulders of his two younger sisters.

She smiled at the two girls. "I was close to their age then and he close to yours when he rode off out of all our lives." Adding, as an afterthought, "I still remember the sad slump of his shoulders as he turned his back on us."

Those fleeting thoughts of his mother and the long-lost older brother she had been so proud of vanished as he sensed a quickening along the precise line of the eager young fellow guardsman.

The gates swung open, and the Sergeant barked the command to march. Pipes squealed to life as the drums struck up a loud tattoo. Marching quickstep behind the band, Matricht passed the Guard box, beside which he would spend many a future hour. That meant little to him now, for all he could see as he stepped through the gateway was the palace and all he could think of was his long-held dreams of guarding with his life, the lives of his king, his queen and his prince and princess.

He had with joy pledged his absolute loyalty to his king and the royal family. It was his sincerest wish that he would somehow matter to his country and his king. He could not have imagined, as he marched the long laneway to the barracks, his gaze still resting on the great stone tower that marked the northern limits of the palace, just how his wish would one day be granted.

Nowhere in his wildest dreams could he have envisioned the events that would engulf him in the shadow of that enormous tower.

3

III. Tower in Front, Tower Behind

The royal palace standing as it was, on a high point of land beside the river, was both the focus of the valley and a sweeping tribute to its history.

Begun a millennium past, it was both a monument to timelessness and a herald to those who had labored to keep it up with the times. To see it was to experience a graphic demonstration of a nation's evolution from the primitive aspect of the ancient and monolithic stone tower of the North Reach down through successively more modern structures to the elegant brick and shining copper spire of the South Reach. Terming it ugly would be to miss the point. To call it beautiful would go too far. It was stately, and in its own way, elegant. It had a self-satisfied look to it that spoke of steadfastness and solidity.

If anyone was to describe the people and the nation that looked to the palace for its guide and rule, there could be a no more fitting symbol. It was indeed, a nation that was steadfast and solid. In fact, it was a nation so imbued with steadfastness and solidity that there was, in all reality, little need for the palace and its court or for the monarch who made his home within it.

There wasn't much for a king to do except show up for some small affairs of state, greet ambassadors, open councils, do some ribbon cutting and sort out the minor quarrels among those attached to his court.

King Rafael the eleventh was a good king. Despite the grandeur of his surroundings, he was a simple man who wanted no more than to be a good ruler to his people and a good husband and father to his family. He loved his wife, the good and gentle Queen Alyssa and doted on his two children, the frail and lovely Princess Emmaline and the energetic and active Prince Micha.

The citizens of the kingdom loved their king and his kind and generous ways. His family, they made uniquely their own. They would revel in the storied mischief of Prince Micha and took a particular interest in the health and well-being of the sweet and fragile Princess Emmaline. They were caring in their affection, so caring, that each day brought a steady parade of well-wishers through the palace gates and into the public courtyard. There, as one, wealthy merchants, ladies of means, delivery boys and serving girls would gather, hoping to catch a glimpse of the royal children. As caring as they were, they were also as generous, indeed so generous that no one left the palace grounds without leaving behind a gift or token of tribute.

King Rafael lived a contented life. Each morning he would rise and bathe, and then, following the custom of the seven previous King Rafaels, the present King Rafael would "take his exercise" by climbing the brass trimmed, cast-iron circular staircase up to the observatory in the South Tower. From this vantage point, he included in the ritual of his daily exercise a survey of his dominion.

From this lofty vantage point, King Rafael could see in vivid detail that he was blessed to be monarch of a truly beautiful and prosperous land. To the east, he could see the river winding its way down past the manicured lawns of the burghers to be lost in the shadows of commercial buildings spread back from the busy harbor. Along the seemingly endless quays, freighters and steamers were loading or unloading. Others, laden with cargo whistled their greetings or farewells to the harbormaster's tower.

To the west, he could look upon the grey, blue of the mountains, rising to white-capped peaks in the far distance. At their feet, he could see a thick apron of forest stretching down to where the smoking factories and mills made a fringe of fuming, busy concrete. Through it all, like glistening strands of a spider web, roads, and streams, alive with traffic carrying the raw products of forest and mine, wormed their way down to the burgeoning maws of mills and smelters.

He could look to the south and see the fertile fields and orchards. The earth was rich and verdant with crops. Like tiny droplets of color against the green backdrop, sheep and cattle grazed their fill on the hillsides. Carts, laden down with the bounty of the earth, made their way to the market areas bordering the royal city.

Looking down, he could see, winding in rows along the crooked streets, or in stately lines along the broad avenues, the homes of the burgers. They all appeared spacious and well maintained. The flow of traffic along the streets was steady. There was no need to look any closer to see that this was a happy and prosperous people.

Taking one last look at the steadily growing crowd of visitors and site-seers gathering before the still closed gates of the palace grounds, he would turn to briefly examine the monolithic rise of unbroken granite that was the inner wall of the North Tower. Afterwards, he retraced his steps down to the ground level and made his way to the dining hall where he would join his wife and children and together, they would sit for breakfast.

Since King Rafael, and the many King Rafael's before him had avoided the dark and difficult stairway up to the North Tower, none of them had ever seen the northern part of their domain. They could not have imagined that beyond the North Tower, there stretched a vast expanse of parched and colorless land. Through the rock-strewn bed of a once large river, a muddy stream in unappealing shades of umber snaked its way through the arid landscape down from the sand hills that marked the horizon. There was no sign of prosperity, no giant smokestacks reaching to the sky, no green, rolling fields, no rich, dark stands of forest. An occasional dark figure scurried along the narrow dusty pathways that strung out in crooked lines between tiny villages huddled near the few patches of faded greenery. Clouds of windblown dust created a dismal scene of unrelenting gloom even under the bright morning sun.

Neither King Rafael nor any of his royal ancestors were foolish men, but they were victims of tradition and an unintentional conspiracy of silence by the populace. They shared a collective blind spot that had developed over the many years and now, was so entrenched that north was little more than an abstract reference on a map. It was as if the northern-most reaches of the kingdom had long ago ceased to exist.

IV. Broom Seller

A s much as this were true for the king and most of his subjects, for those who lived there, the land beyond the North Tower was all too real. It was a chilly and unfriendly land, near barren of life. Most of the plants that grew in the dry and lifeless fields were twisted and thin and devoid of foliage. The land provided the inhabitants with the most meager of livings. They spent their lives in poverty and want. Too proud to go hat in hand to their distant neighbors to the south, too dutiful to seek assistance from the crown, they did what they could to make ends meet. Despite this, they were a resourceful people, able to eke out an existence by the sheer force of their native industriousness, doing whatever they could to earn an honest penny.

Near the banks, of the once great Grande River, where the murky brown stream ran shallow enough to ford, there lived one such family. It was the family of one Ned Norick whose small home stood in the shadow of an ancient stone ruin which legend said was the castle of the last Lord of the North Reaches. Ned's home was a sturdy enough one built at some time in the distant past from stones scrounged from the nearby ruins.

In Ned's father's time, the family had gathered enough material from the ruins to make a small Inn and stable, and he and his family were able to survive by providing refuge and a small measure of provisions for those travelers who passed their way. In the forgotten north, none came to challenge his right to scavenge the castle ruins or make his meager living at its feet.

The living was, indeed meager, for few travelers braved the bleakness of the surrounding country. To supplement this meager income, Ned and his wife made brooms from the reeds that their children gathered along the banks of the nearby stream.

Each week Ned would carry a small parcel of newly made brooms down to the city that surrounded the palace and there, in one of the lesser market squares, under the shadow of the monolithic North Tower, would sell them for a penny or two each. To get the best location to show his wares, he would have to be there very early in the morning. So, on the late eve of market day with his chores around the house done, Ned would set out for the capital.

Somewhere close to the edge of the town, he would find a cozy spot under a stone bridge, or in a hay field, draw his worn blanket over him and sleep until first light. With dawn, he would make his way to the nearest market and find a place among the barrows and stalls to display his wares. Although Ned's brooms had earned the reputation among the market regulars of being sturdy and reliable, there was not a great demand for them.

At the end of the day, Ned would bundle up his remaining brooms and count out the few pennies earned from the sales he had made. Most of the pennies he would put in a small leather purse which he then wrapped up with the brooms. He kept three pennies in his pocket. With two, he would buy himself some stew and a tankard of ale at a local public house.

Having eaten, he would first make his way to the great cathedral that overlooked the clear blue waters of the Western River. Inside, he would drop his third penny into the poor box, light a votive candle and kneel to pray as the last light from the setting sun caught in the colors of the stained glass windows. Then, as the darkness settled over the land, he would rise and start the long journey back home.

Thus it had been for a good many years, for Ned, despite his situation, was of robust health. Yet, as it so happens, even the strongest and healthiest can fall victim to a passing illness and so, Ned found himself confined to bed.

Ned and his family could have weathered this quite well, but it had been a poor season, and few travelers had come by. The family had grown quite dependent on the pennies earned from the sale of the brooms. With Ned not well enough to make the long trek to the city it appeared that he and his family were to be sorely tested. That is, until Roisin, one of Ned's daughters, a quiet girl of some fifteen years, offered to make the trip to the market in his place.

As much as they wanted to refuse, it was evident to Ned and his wife that with their older children's time fully committed at home and the others still very young this was the only recourse open to them. So, it was after much lecturing and warnings to beware the dangers of the city and the possible hazards along the way, permission was grudgingly granted. Roisin sat at the foot of her father's bed as he outlined the course of the enterprise that she was taking on. She listened carefully, pledging to follow his instructions to the letter.

The evening before market day, with a bundle of brooms, bedroll over her shoulder and a few pennies in her tiny leather purse, she bid her family goodbye and set out towards the city. The brooms felt light as feathers as Roisin began to skip joyfully along the dusty road. She could hardly contain her excitement at the adventure that lay before her and hummed a merry tune as she went along.

As the last stray fingers of the setting sun were drawn below the horizon, Roisin's exuberance began to dim. She sang no more merry tunes as the gnarled and twisted trees and boulders along the wayside began to take on a threatening appearance against the darkening sky. Although animal life was scarce in the north, it seemed to Roisin a host of rustling, squeaking, scraping creatures, surrounded her. The pathway itself was hard to see and more than once she stumbled against stones and into potholes nearly falling. Just as it grew too dark for her to continue, she came upon a small circle of trees.

She wrapped herself in her tattered blanket against the cold night air and huddled down as comfortably as she could within the protective ring of trees. The noises of the night continued around her. In her fear and fatigue, the smallest sound, such as the flutter of tiny insect wings, seemed loud and threatening. The starless backdrop became a stage for all sorts of phantasms. She bundled herself into as small a space as possible and waited for the morning. Soon a merciful sleep came over her.

With the first light of dawn, Roisin awoke and breakfasted on a small piece of hard bread and some cold tea. Rested and refreshed as she was, she began to notice the dark and chilling surroundings she had passed through the night before seemed less frightening. She could see greenery; trees spread leafy fingers above her head. Tiny white and purple flowers grew around the edge of the stones. She stepped back onto the path feeling as light of heart as she had been when she first set out. And then, as she rounded a corner she stepped from the tree-cloaked pathway into an open meadow.

She could not hold back a gasp of amazement. The scene that greeted her was more beautiful than any she had ever beheld before. Ahead of her lay the city in its breathtaking enormity. It was alive with more shapes and colors than she had dreamed imaginable. The windows of the many buildings reflected back the dawn light. To Roisin, the city seemed aflame with countless sparkling jewels. For a moment she lost herself in the wonder of it.

Just then a cart passed by and a sharp voice brought her back to reality. "Thoust 'll stand there gawking all morn tide? Some of we be have work to do. Clear the way."

She stepped aside to let the cart pass. Both donkey and old man who rode behind it paid scant attention to her look of awe as she watched them head on intently towards the city. Roisin quickly began to step along behind. As they came closer and closer to the edge of the city, the North Tower, dominating the sky as it did, became more and more imposing. Where others might think it a monstrous eyesore, to Roisin's fresh examination, it was magnificent, almost too wonderful to be believed. When a loose stone on the road nearly sent her sprawling into the back end of the passing cart, she remembered that she was not on a sightseeing journey. She ran up beside of the slow moving cart and called to the hunched over driver. "Excuse me, but could you tell me how to get to the Palisade Street Market?"

A pair of eyes peered out from an old face. " What would ' young thing like thee be doin' out so early not knowin' where

17

is Palisade's Market? I ain't seen thee before, y'ought be home with thy mammar, not talkin' to strangers on't Palisade Rd. Who be ye, anyway, lass?"

As sharp as the tongue was, Roisin detected some gentleness behind it. She told the cart driver of her father and his illness and how she had come to the city in his stead. "So, " said the driver, "Ye be a daughter to Ned o' the Reaches. A fair fine man he is, as I've known him many a year from sharin' sidewalk with him at market. I be Arram, and this be Jezebel," he indicated the donkey with a slow sweep of his arm.

"So ye be takin' your Da's space at Palisades. That's where Jezebel and I be goin'. Follee us, Ned's girl, we'll take thee there. Here", he added, reining the donkey to a stop, "put thy bundles in the cart and hold fast to the sides. I'd take thee to ride beside me, but the poor old Jenny's not so strong as she was."

It was no effort for Roisin to keep up with the old donkey and so; she strode along beside, one hand on the cart. Except to urge the donkey on when it seemed to waver, the old man spoke no further. Still, Roisin felt an air of companionship emanating from him. It buoyed her spirits as they went along.

Once in among the buildings, Roisin realized how lucky she was to have her guide. Within moments, she found herself completely confused by the maze of streets that seemed to her inexperienced eyes to head in all directions. She knew full well that she would have been quickly lost had she dared to make her way through them alone.

The road among the buildings appeared to follow no fixed path but wound this way and that way past doors and windows and under balconies. They seemed to round one corner only to round another in the opposite direction. After what appeared to Roisin to be an endless journey they turned one last corner to where the street widened out into a square. To her amazed senses, this was something magical. Stalls and barrows of all sizes were everywhere to be seen. People scurried intently to and fro among them. Bright banners of all sizes and colors festooned the lampposts around the square. They seemed to fill the sky as they waved in the breeze. The ground floor of the buildings along the perimeter showed gaily decorated open windows. Everywhere she looked, she could see scenes brimming with exotic sights, bright with colors, and alive with movement. So many delicious odors filled her nostrils she paused and breathed deeply to drink it all in. Once again the sharp tone of the cart driver broke through her mesmerized stillness. "There ye go again, lass. Standin' like' t Lord Mayor about to speechify. If thee do not make haste all t' best locations to set up thy wares 'll be gone and ye'll be packin' those same brooms back home wi'out a penny added to thy purse."

Arram quickly led Roisin to a stall hung with bright ribbons on which sat the most beautifully colored bolts of cloth she had ever seen. The fat lady behind the stall surveyed her with a coldly suspicious look, but a short word from the cart driver caused the look to melt away and be replaced with a welcoming smile. As she lay her blanket on the ground and spread out her stock of brooms, she could hear the whispered voices of stall keepers rippling away from her spreading the news about the newcomer in their midst: "Ned o' Reaches daughter. Ned's ill t'home. She's brought's brooms t' sell."

Despite the strangeness of her surroundings, Roisin felt welcomed. Her father, it appeared, was well known and respected by the stall keepers. His daughter was welcome among them. As for Roisin, the day passed as if she was in a dream. As the crowds thinned out, a fat burgher's wife who thought it was just the thing to encourage the neighborhood cats to stay out of her garden purchased the last of her brooms.

With evening, the stall keepers who had seemed all business throughout the day laughed and joked among themselves as they closed up their barrows or packed up their displays. Arram and the fat lady from the cloth stall came to her offering to bring her to the Merchants Inn for a mutton pie, some pudding and a warm glass of Mull before her long trip home. Gratefully she accepted.

In the fading light, she followed old Arram and his donkey Jezebel back towards the edge of the city. They paused with him at the merchant's chapel along the way to light a candle and offer a few prayers of thanksgiving.

So it was, while her father was slowly regaining his strength, Roisin went off to market each week and returned home with the pennies she had earned. The city had become so much a part of her life, that she felt some small dismay at her father's fast returning health. She was becoming aware that her journeys to the city could soon be ending. She began to realize just how much she enjoyed her weekly visit. The colors, the sights, the sounds, the activity, it was all so wonderful, so exciting. It energized her. She knew that she would miss all that, but what troubled her more was that for all the time she had spent there, Roisin had actually seen very little of the city. More than anything, she wanted to explore it. She wanted to see for herself the marvelous sights of the city that she had learned of in bits of conversation overheard from passing shoppers and in the bantering chat of the merchants.

When a time finally came that her father could again shoulder the brooms and walk part way down the path with her as she set upon her journey, Roisin found herself awash in mixed feelings. Happy as she was her father was getting well, she could not avoid a sense of regret he would soon be fit enough to take up the journey himself. She felt both resentment at the approaching loss of a part of her life she had grown quite fond of and a profound sense of guilt for feeling that way.

It was with these thoughts in her mind that Roisin took leave of her father where the path turned away from the dry riverbed. Roisin was not one to burden herself in gloom. The unfriendly land where she made her home was gloomy enough. The evening was fair, and soon her spirits rose. Unlike on her first trip to the city, the dark pathway no longer held any terror for her. It was a tired, but contented Roisin who spread out her blanket in the circle of trees with its welcome embrace had become her regular stopping place. It was a sweet and dreamless sleep that carried her through the few remaining hours of darkness and into the golden dawn of a new day.

Although she no longer needed his guidance, Roisin waited at the edge of the city until old Arram and Jezebel rattled into view. Together they would make their way through the early morning streets to the busy market square.

As she had each morning as she entered the city, Roisin would look up at the dark face of the North Tower. The awe she felt when first she looked upon it had turned to a respectful familiarity. As close as she felt she was to it, she had never, in fact, been near the palace. She knew nothing of the splendidly beautiful South Tower except what she had heard indirectly from those around her in the market. Even in a city so enamored of its royal family, the palace was not a common subject of conversation in the busy marketplace.

All Roisin really knew was that she wanted to see the palace close up, perhaps even catch a fleeting glimpse of the Princess, or even the King himself. The palace began to dominate her thoughts as she went mechanically about the business of setting up her merchandise. If she could only get to see the palace, just once, she thought, she would then gladly give the marketing task back to her father. She knew the chance was slight. Her time would soon be over, and the income from the brooms was too precious to her family to allow her time to slip away from her display for even a few minutes. But the palace called to her and more than once that day, she turned her eyes upward to look at the North Tower brooding on the hill so near and yet so far away.

5

V. Foresters

Older and stockier than at the time of his fatal encounter with Colonel Nevil and his niece, but still as cold and arrogant, Leonis sat, tilted back on the huge oaken chair, his riding boots, crossed at the ankle atop the thick, ancient wood table. Behind him, a giant tapestry of a great cat springing, its forelegs outstretched, claws bared, its teeth white against the tawny background signifying his heritage and power. He was, after all, the Grand Duke Leonis of the West March and battle chieftain of his nation.

He had gained his title at an early age, when his father, the previous Grand Duke, and to the present Duke's mind, a somewhat simple and pedestrian man, was kicked in the head by a frightened goat. Although Leonis loved his father in his own way, he had to laugh every time he remembered it. He could still see it in his mind's eye; The cantankerous goat in his father's beloved flower patch, his father diving to catch the goat before it completely ruined the Geraniums or whatever, grabbing it by its tiny tail and for his efforts, receiving a fierce kick between his astonished eyes.

The sharp hoof of the goat penetrated his skull and sent shards of bone deep into the late Duke's brain. It was all so ludicrous. Just thinking about it, Leonis couldn't stop the guffaw. " We should seek out a similar goat for our, insipid, oh, I'm sorry, our beloved King," Leonis intoned to no one in particular through his laughter.

"I beg your pardon, highness," asked the elderly knight seated on the bench to his right.

"Oh, it was nothing, Stanley, I may have just burped."

The Grand Duke had spoken, and it was enough for Sir Stanley. He, like all the other men in the room, was totally loyal to his liege, the Grand Duke Leonis.

Most of the men present had some history with the West March. They were aristocratic subjects, former members of the now defunct Ranger and Berserker regiments and a number of others who were attracted to the duke's hard and arrogant personality.

Sir Stanley made an ideal front for these men who were all members in good standing of the West March Foresters. While Sir Stanley was proud of his status as commander of the West March Foresters, he believed that this group with its regular monthly trek through the villages and towns of the West March was essentially an honorific position granted for good service.

As far as Sir Stanley knew, they would ride the monthly parade through the villages and towns of the West March, showing the Duke's colors to the peasantry, then return to Castle Leonis for a medieval feast of roast venison followed by endless tankards of ale in the winter court. After that, Sir Stanley would return home, escorted by a couple of his Lieutenants whose real job it was to make sure the besotted old man didn't fall off his horse on the way.

Sir Stanley was an excellent figurehead for the Foresters, a true member of the gentry. And apparently happy enough, and dim enough to think that his role and his patrol squadron of Foresters was a nicely symbolic exercise to parade out once a month.

With Sir Stanley dropping into bed in a drunken stupor, much to the dismay of his wife who believed it was undignified for someone of his status, the Forester escort would hasten back to Castle Leonis to learn of the more practical duties for which they truly served the Grand Duke.

With the return of Sir Stanley's escort to the winter court, the tones of revelry and conversation changed.

Leonis, once more rocking on the giant oaken chair, nonchalantly picking his teeth with a small dagger loved these moments. He loved this room, 'The Winter Court', with its gigantic fireplace, it's array of heavy tables and benches, the especially huge oaken table before him, and the enormous oaken chair in which he sat. There was just enough room for the forty-five Regulars, men of the Foresters to sit comfortably facing their leader.

The cooking and serving staff had been sent home shortly after the departure of Sir Stanley, but not before setting out several hogsheads of ale tapped, and ready for pouring. The cleaners would not be coming until the early hours of the morning.

Now they could all get down to the task at hand, expressing their hatred of the King. How they despised the weak and peaceful Monarch. How they craved to extend their power and how they truly believed that Grand Duke Leonis would be a far better king because he wouldn't be pussy footing around those wastefully independent neighboring states. Why should the West March end at the Horne River when it could be extended into the Principality of Durain and reach at least to the mountains if not all the way to the coast?

Relaxed and somewhat in his cups, this is the time when Leonis would air his personal grievances with the King. "That damn Rafael," he would groan, "how many times have I dropped into the palace to meet on some important business only to put it off to join him and his insufferable family as they jogged up those endless stairs to the south tower's observation deck. Damned daily constitutional, that's what he called it.

"The idiot," Leonis would sneer, "he surveys his domain while his family waves to the crowd of adoring subjects gathered outside the gate to watch this simple-minded spectacle. It's ridiculous. He looks south and east and west and so assumes everything is in order. But that idiot has no idea that the Grande River of the North has become nothing more than a tiny, muddy trickle, leaving most of the land parched and dry and the people in the villages and towns along its banks starved and frustrated and hopefully, ready to rebel. But not yet."

The Duke slammed the forelegs of his huge chair to the ground and stabbed the armrest with the small dagger that had been his toothpick. It stood straight up amidst the numerous scars of its many earlier encounters.

Working the blade free, Leonis continued his rant, one that was very familiar to his band of henchmen he called his Foresters, "Those impoverished fool Northerners; they are still rather tame. Just like everyone else in this dreary country, they are still infected by this bizarre national love affair with the royal family. We still have much work to do to continue to encourage the spirit of rebellion among them."

Leaning forward and drawing all eyes towards him, Leonis

began to speak in a crisper more businesslike tone, "Over the next few weeks, Arve and his group will ride to the North Reaches and test the waters, so to speak. He and his men will work their ways to stir the people up against the king. After all, as far as they know, he has forgotten them among their dead fields and their pitiful mud puddles. Find us some allies there, Arve."

Decked out in the military look of the Foresters ceremonial uniform, Arve, a former captain of the disbanded Rangers, gave off an air of cruelty. His eyes were passionless, his goateed face chiseled and angular. He nodded to Leonis, his hand rising in a crisp salute, and then he turned to the crowd, indicating those of his personal associates among them and called out, Gentlemen we meet at the crossroads on the border's edge tomorrow at dawn. We will set out our plans tomorrow as we ride."

"Sire, " said Arve speaking directly to Leonis as his men gathered round him, " we take our leave now that we might quickly set out to do your bidding."

Leonis made a slight nod and Arve and his troop left the Winter Court and headed off into the night. With Arve and his group gone, the others began to drift away. Leonis called out to one of them, "Karl, a moment."

A balding, unimposing man of uncertain age stepped out toward him. "Your highness?" His voice rising in a questioning intonation.

As if he had not heard Karl's voice, the Duke proceeded. "You know the city, Karl. I want you and your staff to be on the lookout for any unobtrusive way into the palace. Be sure the Guards are unaware of your digging around.

"Yes Highness, but as their commander and chief could you not just have them look the other way?"

27

"Perhaps, but I have my doubts about that, the Guard is too devoted to their duties and too fiercely loyal to the King. If it were the Rangers or Berserkers, it might be possible. But, no, Karl, our investigations must be subtle, and, if we can't get in, how are we to find out when and where the King will be when he goes out. It has to be something different, something where he is vulnerable, and there are not too many eyes watching him, Guard or civilian.

"Certainly, highness, you have a time frame in mind?"

"First let us gather what information we can. There will be plenty of time for time frames then. If nothing else, Karl, you well know that I am a patient man."

Karl may well have known no such thing, but he bowed his head, "As you wish, Highness, my eyes, and ears are ready to serve you."

"Good man, Karl, Keep me posted regarding your progress."

Karl bowed, backed away and left. Leonis and his personal guards were the only ones remaining in the Winter Court. "I would love to stay here," he said to no one in particular, "but the bed chambers are too, damn drafty. Ah well, Duchess Elspeth awaits me in the townhouse, so let's be off."

Hardly a townhouse, the home of the Grand Duke Leonis was the second largest building in the city, second only to the massive and mostly uninhabited Palace itself.

It may have been the place Duke Leonis lived most of the time; it was, in reality, Duchess Elspeth's home. I was too domestic for Leonis. The rooms were filled with her frilly geegaws and her collectibles, and of course, there were the gardens, and among them, the fatal garden of the goat where, to the present Duke's mind, his far too domesticated father met a tragic, if somewhat comical end, over a few stupid flowers.

28

The Grand Duke's heart, although there were many who doubted that such an organ existed, belonged to the ancient stone walls, the courts, and keeps of Castle Leonis standing in place on the edge of the protected forest of the Great West March.

It was there, an hour's gallop from the city that Leonis met with his associates, planned his devious plans and dreamed his dream of reviving the Ranger and Berserker regiments. Most importantly, it was where he made plans for claiming the crown and overthrowing all those insipid non-aggression pacts that had turned the nations of the sub-continent soft and weak-kneed and all due to the urging of the softest, most weak-kneed, and most annoying of them all, King Rafael. In the cruel and acquisitive eyes of Duke Leonis, Rafael was the most unworthy of leaders.

"Karl is a good man. He'll find a way," were Leonis' final thoughts as he fell into a deep, relaxed sleep. He was content in the knowledge that Karl and his staff would do everything they could to assist him in ridding himself and the country of King Rafael the soft and weak-kneed.

In the morning, Leonis had an appointment with the commandant of the palace guard. That meant another futile run up that glass enclosed stairway to wave and be waved at by the masses of citizenry and the insufferable tourists who would gather at the gate each morning in hopes of getting a glimpse of the King, or even better, the Queen and the royal children.

"There will be no more of that when I wear the crown, " mumbled the sleeping Leonis.

6

VI. Through the Gates

Sometimes fate takes strange turns. This day, Roisin's brooms were in high demand. When the last one was gone, and the pennies secured in the leather purse, the best part of the day still remained. Roisin took it as a miracle not to be questioned. She gathered up her belongings. Looking around the marketplace, she could see it was also a bountiful day for the other merchants. They were all too busy with customers to chat with her. She came to a quick decision and waving goodbye to the nearby merchants, set off with a bouncing step, to explore the city and, once and for all, have a good close look at the palace.

Strolling happily up the Palisades Road, Roisin began to realize the riches she thought that she had seen in the marketplace and the surrounding homes were nothing compared to what she now encountered. As she got nearer to the palace, the houses began to change. They no longer stood side by side, but were larger and surrounded by colorful gardens with lawns and trees clipped to a near dreamlike perfection. Shops and even taverns had an air of gentility that she had not seen before. Fewer people walked the streets, but the carriages were more plentiful. Then, as if she had passed through an invisible gateway, the appearances of the houses changed again. To her eyes, these houses set well back from the roadway, each surrounded by vast park-like gardens and bordered by wrought iron fences were more beautiful than she had imagined a house could possibly be. Few carriages and fewer pedestrians made their way along the street, and Roisin began to feel uncomfortable. It was almost as if she was violating the peaceful elegance by her presence. More than once she hesitated, nearly turning and racing back to the relative safety of the noisy and common marketplace. But, she was determined to have a good close look at the palace and so, she continued.

The Palisades Road came to an abrupt end at a broad and busy thoroughfare. Unlike the silent street she had just left, this one, much wider than the former, had a more familiar feel. The traffic, the bustle, the many colored flags that danced in the breeze along the road's edge, made it seem more like the marketplace to Roisin. There was an almost tangible feeling of joy and excitement emanating from the multitudes on foot and in carriages making their way along the broad stretch of road.

Although Roisin did not know it at the time, this was Coronation Lane. It was the path that over the centuries had witnessed the quiet predawn ride of the crown prince from the palace to the cathedral and later that same day shook to the vibration of the cheering masses that formed to salute the newly crowned king returning to the palace to take his place as sovereign. There he would sit in state upon the royal throne overlooking the Grand Hall of the Palace, and down through the main gates to this self-same road.

If any road was to be the heart of a kingdom, this was it.

And like a heart, it pulsed with life. Almost unconsciously, Roisin joined with the traffic on Coronation Lane and was carried along up the hill towards the palace. So intense was the flow, she barely had the opportunity to glance at the marvels surrounding her. The parks, the gardens, the buildings of state resplendent in flags and banners were little more than a blur to her.

Roisin was so completely overwhelmed by all the unfamiliar sights and sounds she hardly noticed that the upward flow had stopped. She might have stayed where she was for hours, lost in a dazed cloud of exhilaration, had the woman beside her not spoken. "It's remarkable, don't you think? Have you ever seen such beautiful stone work?"

Only then did Roisin take notice of her surroundings. She was standing with a group of people at the palace gate. The massive doors, covered with an eye-dazzling array of brass and wrought iron ornamentation, were flung open. Overhead, a colossal stone portal, covered with grimacing gargoyles directed the eye along the convolution of line and shape towards the palace grounds. Together they framed the palace garden. On either side, soldiers in the black trimmed Whites of the Royal Guard stood at rigid attention, the silver of their plumed helmets glistening in the afternoon sun. Their rifles, braced against the efficient looking unadorned black leather of their bandoleers, seemed in perpetual salute to the enormous structure behind them. Their eyes, looking at no one, saw everyone.

Almost imperceptibly, the group of people moved forward. Roisin would never know if it was the surge of the crowd or her own curiosity that took her along with them. As she came abreast of the guardsman, she felt a moment of panic, expecting the shining bayonet to drop down suddenly and block her way.

The guardsman remained immobile, the bayonet forming part of an arch above her head as she passed through the gates and into the palace grounds.

If the market on Palisade Road had a carnival atmosphere, the atmosphere in the palace grounds although similarly electrifying, was quite different. It felt to Roisin as if the joyous spirit of Easter and the warm kinship of Christmas had joined together and taken on substance. There was a definite feeling of festiveness, but with the kind of restrained decorum of a christening or wedding. The crowds exuded a quiet enthusiasm as they passed among the carefully kept hedgerows and flowerbeds. While most eyes looked upwards towards the great glass windowed observatory several floors above, Roisin's eyes absorbed the sense of quality and wealth that pervaded the crowd. They seemed to drink in the beauty of the landscaped gardens. When someone called out, "I see her, I see Emmaline. Look! The window just to the right of the balcony!"

The crowd seemed to move as one towards the palace wall, their eyes searching against the reflection of the afternoon sun upon the observatory windows, to catch a glimpse of their monarch's beloved daughter. Roisin looked up long enough to catch a glimpse of a girl about her own age waving down at her. As the crowd broke into spontaneous applause, Roisin noted, even from that distance, the delicacy and frailty of the tiny figure so high above. Then, her attention was drawn away from the crowd and towards the most amazing sight anyone from so impoverished a background as she might ever behold.

Along the wall off to the right of the grand doorways where the crowd had gathered, Roisin could see, neatly laid out in rows, the accumulation of gifts the day's visitors to the palace grounds had brought as tributes for their honored king and his esteemed family. Many of these gifts were clearly of inestimable value, and to Roisin, immeasurable beauty. They drew Roisin to them like a moth to a flame.

What wonders there were! Artifacts of polished silver and gold, exotic wood carvings, precious cloth beyond any she had seen at the market, Instruments for making music, paintings and sculpture, items of furniture that in their beauty belied their efficiency and comfort and the more varied and exquisite array of toys than Roisin could have imagined even in her wildest dreams. There was everything from delicately life-like porcelain dolls and hand carved hobbyhorses to wagons and tin whistles. Hypnotized by the sheer variety and richness of everything, Roisin walked among the rows of gifts, examining everything as if with brand new eyes.

Overwhelmed by it all as she was, Roisin failed to note the trumpet calls from the parapet, or see the crowd filter slowly and somewhat regretfully through the gates and back out to join the homeward bound traffic of Coronation Lane. Enraptured by all she saw around her, she did not hear the great gates clang shut. Seated among a coterie of dolls and stuffed animals unlike any she had seen before, Roisin neither noticed the two guardsmen, who with swords in hand, walked among the rows of tributes, nor they, her. Not looking for the likes of a ragged girl who was little more than a child, they passed her by unheedingly and were soon out of sight on their way back to barracks.

After sundown, most of the items left in tribute by the visitors to the palace grounds would be collected by the palace staff and put into storage where they could be evaluated. Many would be returned to the marketplace to fund the children's hospitals throughout the land. Others would be sent to museums and art galleries. Many others became special gifts for visiting dignitaries and their families while a few remained to be used and enjoyed by the court. Still others would be stored away against a time when there might be a need for them, or until someone figured out for what they might be needed.

Despite a very strict policy on the treatment of the tributes that were added daily to the Royal Stores, King Rafael had judged it fitting that the prince and princess should have the opportunity to survey the daily collection that they might, in some small way, enjoy the generosity of their doting subjects. If some small item struck their fancy, and was deemed suitable, then they might keep it. So it was, the Royal heirs were permitted the privilege of being the first to examine the rows of treasures great and small.

Inside the palace, their daily studies done, Emmaline and Micha happily prepared to reclaim their gardens from the day's crowds of well-wishers. It had become a regular tradition for them to wait in the upper hall until the guards had done their walk-through searching for stragglers. When the garden was clear, they would make their way down a side staircase through the pages' entrance and into the grounds. They would then walk among the rows of tributes, enjoying the beautiful, laughing at the odd and funny and, if they could, trying out the functional. For Emmaline especially, it provided a few moments to be herself and free of the awesome responsibility her position put upon her. The antics of the ever-exuberant Micha striking an exaggerated pose with some odd, or mysterious item taken from the surrounding piles might even draw a gentle giggle from her.

Even then, there was a certain formality to her step as she followed the rambunctious Micha, whose path led him over and through the mountains of artifacts more than it did along the neat pathways between them. This day, there seemed to be more of the odd and ridiculous than usual. Micha postured and Emmaline laughed. Encouraged by this, Micha became more boisterous, and skipped from item to item trying to draw more of the rare laughter from his sister. Spotting what he thought was a large rag doll on the other side of one of the rows, he jumped over, ready to grab it and send it flying back through the air to Emmaline.

7

VIII. New Friends

Roisin was filled with horror at the unexpected arrival of the laughing-faced boy. She froze, speechless as his laughter cut short.

Sizing up the girl confronting him, Micha knew this was no rag doll, nor was she likely an assassin. He had never seen such a look of surprise and terror from anyone. Before he could react, Roisin turned to run, only to find herself face to face with another, this time a girl close to her own age. Roisin had never before felt so totally alone and helpless. Trembling with fear, she lowered her eyes and wiped her hand across her face, leaving a smear of tears. But where she had expected a sharp retort, she was amazed at the gentility of the voice that came from the girl who faced her. "You needn't be afraid. We shan't hurt you."

Perhaps if Roisin had known to whom she was speaking, she would have been overcome with awe. As it was, the stranger's voice calmed her. She tried to explain herself in a still shaking voice, "I was looking at all the beautiful things. I didn't mean any harm."

At that moment, she realized that the crowds were gone and the palace gates in the distance were firmly shut. A deeper feeling of fear and despair came over her as she realized she was locked inside the palace grounds. First, she wondered how she would get home, then certain that the two before her would turn her in to the guards, she began to wonder what was going to happen to her. A confusion of thoughts filled her head when, almost as if she had read her mind, the girl before her spoke again. "Don't be afraid, we shan't tell the guards that you're here."

"We shan't tell the guards!" echoed Micha in amazement.

"No we shan't." said Emmaline with the same kind of firm tone Micha had heard his father use when issuing a court decision. Surprised as he was at this, Micha knew that Emmaline would allow no resistance. He then relaxed. The matter had been taken out of his hands and he stood waiting to find out what his sister had planned.

For a brief moment, the two girls gazed curiously at each other. Roisin looked at Emmaline and saw her quiet elegance, her frail beauty, the signs of a life free from hardship and material wants. Emmaline looked at Roisin and saw the tiredness of unrelenting poverty, the bitterness of want, the defiant pride of one who worked hard for anything she had. These first impressions were quickly passed over, as each girl found in the gaze of the other something familiar. They shared a feeling of pride in themselves and their family. They both felt intensely the heavy burden of responsibility that their state in life had placed on them. They recognized in each other a sensitivity and gentleness of nature that had stood them apart from those around them and instilled in each of them a sense of loneliness. That sense of loneliness had prevented either girl from developing any really close friendships. This shared sense of loneliness struck a harmonic chord in both of them. In that instant, a bond was formed between the two girls.

So complete was the bond, that within moments of the traumatic discovery, the two girls were chatting as if they had known each other all their lives. Micha was dumbfounded, his sister, usually so aloof and intense, was giggling and laughing as she spoke. He had never heard her talk so much.

Hiding a feeling of embarrassment, Micha shrugged his shoulders and turned awkwardly away from the two girls on the pretense of examining a very stylized ivory carving of an elephant atop a coat rack of some sort.

Sensing his discomfort, the two girls joined him in his examination and within seconds, Micha was his old self. Having an audience of two for his clowning appealed to Micha. The stranger laughed easily and this pleased him no end. Together the three continued their review of the piles of tributes. It was not Princess Emmaline, Prince Micha and Roisin Norick the peasant from the North Reaches, but Emma, Mitch and Rosie who talked and laughed together like the oldest and truest of friends. This could have gone on indefinitely when the sudden, ear-splitting boom of a cannon stopped them short.

Roisin looked around in dismay. She recognized that cannon-ade. Usually, she heard it as she left the city on her way home from the market. It signaled the end of the day. A sense of panic once again overwhelmed her. Her face went ashen. Seeing this Emmaline reached over and touched Roisin's sleeve. "What's wrong, Rosie?"

"Oh, Emma," sobbed Roisin, "What is to become of me. Will I ever get home?"

"Of course you will," said Emmaline with an imperial certainty that belied her true feelings.

"Where do you live?" asked Micha.

For some unknown reason, Roisin felt hesitant about providing that information, but Micha's inquiring look called for some sort of a response. She gestured vaguely towards the North Tower and tried to speak in the most casual way she could, "Oh, near the Palisades Market just beyond the North Tower."

Micha puzzled a moment then smiled. "Don't worry, Rosie, I know a secret way out to Palisades Road not too far from the North Tower. "His words were punctuated by the approaching clatter of marching boots. "Come on, let's get moving; the Evening Guard is taking the watch. They'll find us for sure if we stick around here."

Following Micha's lead, the girls began to run using the trees and shrubbery to conceal their movements from the guards. As they approached the wall, Roisin began to notice that Emmaline was slowing. Her labored breathing sounding clearly above the distant shouts of the guardsmen as they took their station. She recognized immediately that Emmaline was experiencing difficulty and stopped her.

Wheezing and panting, Emmaline covered her mouth to smother the sounds of a cough. Roisin put her arm around her shoulder to steady her. Micha, running on ahead, realized that he was alone and turned back to confront the two girls. "Come on," he said, "let's go. The guards will find us."

"I don't think that Emma can keep up," said Roisin firmly and she turned to put her hands on Emmaline's shoulders and looked steadily into her eyes. "You mustn't go any further. Don't worry; Mitch will take me. You must rest a few moments and then go back home. The night air is too hard on you."

With a heartfelt goodbye, Roisin turned towards Micha who

stood nearby, an expression of agitation darkening his face. "Come on, "said Micha, "let's go!"

Roisin nodded, then turned to smile weakly at Emmaline. Emmaline, who had gained control over her wheezing, smile weakly back. "Will you come again, Rosie?" she asked plaintively.

In that instant, Roisin knew that she would have to see Emma again. When that might be, she could not imagine. "I'm not sure," she said, shaking her head sadly. "If I'm still bringing brooms to sell at the market next week, I'll try to come.

The marching and the shouting came from quite close by. Micha grabbed Roisin by the hand and began to pull her along. As they ran, Roisin noticed that the gardens began to take on a look of neglect. The palace walls had undergone a subtle change. As amazingly beautiful as it still seemed to Roisin, it lacked the look of airy elegance that marked the front of the palace. The windows were smaller and deeply recessed into the stone walls. Had she time to study it more carefully, she would have seen the structure of the palace become more primitive in appearance. Where there had been fine brickwork and delicately wrought iron the palace was now a crude construction of stone and timber.

There was little time to ponder these changes as Micha grabbed her hand again and pulled her quickly to the left and through a small dark doorway. Narrow dust covered stone tables, lined the dimly lit walls. In the sparse light, she could see on the wall carved images of knights and ladies. Although beyond her experience, Roisin gasped in understanding. Micha had brought her into a burial vault. Without giving her a chance to express her dismay, he led her towards one of the images on the wall. She vaguely noticed that this one was different from the others. This one was neither lady, nor knight, but a wild-eyed satyr. "Don't worry," said Micha, his voice echoing among the stones, "Whoever built this particular burial site had other plans."

He pushed his fingers into the satyr's eyes and pulled. With a creak, it swung towards his pull revealing a dark passageway beyond. "Follow the passageway a short distance. You'll come out behind a small shrine. If you follow the line of bushes to your right, it will bring you out onto the street. I think its Palisades Road. Good luck, Rosie. If I see you again, I'll tell you how I found out about this."

Micha half pushed Roisin through the doorway and before she knew it, he had shut the heavy door behind her. For a brief moment, she felt a tingling of horror. Had the boy left her here to die? A glimpse of light in the near distance quickly put that thought behind her as she headed towards it. The light came from around the edges of a large stone that slid easily to the side as she pushed it. With a step, she was outside the palace wall. She barely noticed the rock slip back into place as she looked out from around the stone and mortar grotto towards the street. She thought she recognized it as the one she had been on earlier in the day.

In the fading light of evening, she could see pedestrians passing by. Waiting until she was sure no one was looking, Roisin slipped from behind the statue and quickly fell to her knees in front of it. No one would pay any attention to a merchant girl who had stopped to pray at the shrine of St Dymphna. Hesitating a moment where she knelt, Roisin breathed a quick prayer of thanksgiving, and then was back on the Palisades Road and on her way.

The marketplace was dark and nearly empty. Except for

some street sweepers and the sound of laughter issuing from the Merchants' Public House as she passed by, there was no sign of life.

After having seen the sights of Coronation Lane and been in the palace grounds, Roisin was acutely aware of the smallness of the market square and the tawdriness of the surrounding buildings. The houses she passed by on the way out of the city seemed terribly tiny and poorly cared for. In contrast, Roisin's high spirits cultured everything around her with a feeling of warmth and charm.

As she went by the tiny merchants' chapel at the edge of town, she could see in the distance the donkey cart bouncing along, the thin, shapeless form of the aged driver buried inside his large cloak bent over the reins. Roisin knew that she could easily catch up, but held back, reluctant to risk breaking the spell her afternoon's adventure had cast upon her. This turned out to be a needless worry, for when at last she did catch up to old Arram, he was his usual taciturn self. He returned her casual greeting in his usual style. "Thou wast gone early from Market, m'lass. Dids't see aught of the city?"

Although his words were framed as a question, the old man neither sought nor expected an answer. Roisin, recognizing this, walked silently along beside the cart until they reached the place where their paths divided. She reached her hand out to scratch Jezebel's ear and looked up at the old man. "My father is better, now. He may come next week instead of me."

That was Roisin's goodbye. Arram's wrinkled face showed no sign of emotion. He nodded vaguely in Roisin's direction, then gathered his cloak about him more tightly and gently snapped the reins. "Get on, Jezebel."

As the cart pulled away from Roisin, the old man turned in

his seat to face her and nodded gravely. "Farewell to thee, Lady Roisin of the nor' Reaches," he said, and then turning back, was on his way, and soon hidden from Roisin's sight by the trees.

She paused a moment to ponder the strange formality of his farewell, then brushed it aside and headed off along the path for home. Her spirits were buoyant. She almost skipped along the pathway. Her thoughts were still back at the palace. Over and over again in her head, she went through the details of her encounter with her two new acquaintances. She thought of how easy it was to speak to the girl she knew as Emma. Roisin who had never had a real friend in her life, could not help but marvel over the mysterious sense of kinship she felt with the two palace children, and especially with Emma. It was as if she had known her forever and yet, she realized, she did not know her at all.

Roisin tried to construct a history for the two as she went along. Perhaps they were the children of the cook, or of one of the servants or, although Roisin could hardly consider the possibility, perhaps they were children of one of the courtiers. Why their father might be one of the royal guards, or their mother one of the ladies in waiting. Roisin liked this the best. She like it because it made her new-found friends special and they did so feel to her like special friends. So deeply engrossed was she in these pleasant thoughts, she did not even think of the very real possibility that she would never see them again. Not until the next morning as she neared her home, did it occur to her that she might never again go back to the city.

8

VIII. Worry

A feeling of sadness slowed her step. Even the warmth of her mother's welcoming greeting and the delicious scents of the morning meal that awaited her could not raise her spirits. Her gloom was complete when her mother told her, "Your father wishes to speak to you as soon as you have finished eating."

Back in the palace, Emmaline had found it difficult to sleep. Her thoughts were full of the mysterious girl she and Micha had met in the garden that afternoon. Although she had no idea who she was or where she lived, she knew she wanted to see her again. Never before had she felt so comfortable with someone, so able to laugh, so ready to talk. Although she knew she might never see the girl again, she wanted so much to see and talk to her. She could hardly wait for the week to pass. So distracted was she, even the King commented to his wife upon it. "Emmaline doesn't quite seem to be herself these days. Perhaps we should call the physician to look at her."

Queen Alyssa smiled at her husband. She was touched by his concern but shook her head. She didn't know what was bothering Emmaline, but she did somehow recognize it was not something the stodgy old royal physician could treat.

Despite being his normal mischievous self, Prince Micha, too, thought about the girl in the courtyard. Their flight from the guards had been an exciting and exhilarating experience for him. He associated Roisin with adventure and hoped she would come again. So enthused was he with the possibility, he spent the week inspecting the palace grounds for new escape routes.

Far beyond the shadow of the North Tower, in a house of scavenged stones close by the all but dried up river, Roisin had finished her morning meal and was making her way towards the stables where her father was waiting. She could not put away the feeling of dread she harbored for the expected words of her father.

As soon as he saw Roisin, Ned stopped his work and walked toward her. He gestured toward two large stones indicating that she sit down. As she did, he sat down across from her and leaned towards her. She could not raise her face to look at him, but instead, allowed her gaze to wander over the hard brown, almost lifeless soil at her feet.

Roisin sank deeper and deeper into her misery as her father spoke. "As you know, Little Rose, your mom and I, we were awful worried about sending you to the city while I was ill. You seem to have done better than we ever could have imagined. We know you're a dutiful girl, but you took on this job and have carried it out with Norick pride, for sure.

Now, you know we said you would do this for as long as I was ill and unable to go myself. Well, truth be told, I'm well enough now to take on this task again."

"Oh," thought Roisin, sinking even deeper in gloom, "here it comes."

"But," Ned continued, "I have plenty to do around here and you have done so well selling our brooms…. Well, I hate to put this on you, but could you continue bringing the brooms to market, at least until the weather turns cold? I know it's a lot to expect of one so young and it's true your mother, and I will both worry about you until you're home. But, please consider it."

Ned leaned even closer to Roisin who said nothing for a moment. Her mind was working trying to unscramble what her father had said from what she had expected him to say. For Ned, the hesitation seemed to imply some serious doubt on Roisin's part. Needless to say, he was surprised, when with a squeal of joy she rushed to grab him around the neck and hold him in the fiercest, longest, most joyous hug he had received from her since she was a small child. "Then you will do it?" he mumbled through his consternation.

Speechless, Roisin nodded her head up and down and planted a kiss on her father's cheek. Before he could say anything, she had broken free and was skipping across the yard towards the house. Ned, with a look of sheer amazement, watched her go, his hand coming up to touch his cheek where seconds before his daughter had kissed him. Scratching his head in puzzlement, he made his way back to the stable and his work.

She tried her best to keep busy and distracted from thoughts of her next trip to the city, but the days crawled by for Roisin. When the time came, at last, to set off, she could barely stand still long enough for her father to tie on her pack of brooms before she skipped off along the trail. She flew along the path as if on a cloud of air. By the time she reached the little circle of trees she was so giddy with excitement at the prospect of seeing her two friends from the palace garden she could not sleep.

9

IX. Fortune Smiles

Before the sun had done little more than stretch out tiny wisps of pink and pale gold along the line of the horizon, Roisin was back on the pathway. The city was still dark when she reached the fork in the road where she would join Arram and Jezebel. She sat on a large flat stone near the edge of the road. Her sandaled feet kept up an agitated tapping as she waited. She could feel the dampness of the grass through the coarse wool of her stockings.

For the first time since the journey had begun the previous night, she felt the weight of the brooms on her shoulders. She was thinking the sun would never rise when a sliver of sunlight peeked over the horizon to emphasize the dark and forbidding aspect of the massive North Tower.

The sight of what was the most dismal section of the great palace, was enough to fan the already blazing flames of impatience that Roisin felt She could wait no longer for old Arram. She was on her feet and making haste towards the still darkened buildings of the city.

When she reached the marketplace, the square glistened in

the first silver glow of day. A few of the merchants, those selling farm produce, were wheeling their barrows into place and set up their displays, but mostly, the market square was empty. Roisin entertained the prospect of finding a more advantageous location to set up her display but decided against it.

By the time the other merchants had made their way to the square and set up their wares for the day's selling, Roisin had been able to catch a few moments sleep. Her little nap had gone some way to make up for the restless night she had spent. She felt refreshed as she stretched and opened her eyes. There was Jezebel right beside her munching on some hay that old Arram had put down for her. She reached over and stroked the old donkey's ear, and Jezebel responded with a contented nicker. Old Arram was about his business and cast not so much as a glance at Roisin.

When she approached him to say good morning, he greeted her as he always did, then asked, with some concern in his voice, "Thy Da's still sick abed?"

Roisin explained the family decision to have her continue coming to the market for the time being. Arram nodded with satisfaction. If he was curious why she had not met him at the fork in the road, as usual, he showed no sign.

To Roisin, the morning dragged on and on. The crowds swirled around her, but she was indifferent to them. The shoppers who came to look at her display she treated with an off-handed courtesy. That could have caused lost sales for someone of a sourer disposition, but despite her impatience and distraction, her sunny nature shone through. Only someone who knew her well would recognize that she was not her usual self.

An eternity seemed to have passed when the bells of the giant cathedral peeled across the city announcing to all it was noon. Roisin was too anxious to eat, and there were still brooms left to be sold, so she stayed at her display as the lunchtime shoppers made their way through the market stalls. As noon edged into the afternoon, Roisin was feeling a sense of despondency tugging at the corners of her mind. There were too many brooms still left unsold, and she realized the importance of every penny she could earn. She knew she must remain in the marketplace as long as there was even the slightest hope she could make those further sales. And, if that were the case, she knew there would be little time left to get to the palace before the gates closed.

Then, as if in answer to her unspoken prayer, a strange thing happened. An elegant and wealthy woman accompanied by two young men, both loaded down with parcels stopped in front of Roisin's tiny sales area. She did not approach but coolly examined both Roisin and the brooms. She stood a moment and then spoke a word to one of the young men. He put down the parcels he was carrying and walked up to Roisin. "Madam wishes to know if these brooms are handmade," he asked in a tone he used with those he felt were his social inferiors.

Roisin looked at the young man, then at her display of brooms, then past him to the wealthy lady where she stood. Just one look at the brooms would tell anyone with half a sense that the brooms could not be other than homemade. She was about to tell the young man so in no uncertain terms, but then thought better of it and nodded yes. The young man turned back towards his mistress and echoed Roisin's nod. Had she been watching; she would have seen the elegant lady make a slight incline of her head. As it was, she was unprepared for what happened then. The young man turned back to her, his hand reaching into a large purse he wore on his belt as he spoke. "Madam will take all you have," and he dropped a number of coins in front of Roisin.

"Are these them all," he asked his tone curt as he swept up all the brooms and tossed them onto his shoulder.

Before Roisin could reply, the young man had returned to the elegant lady, picked up the other parcels from the ground where he had set them, and the three were gone. Roisin picked up the coins the young man had dropped. There were more than enough to cover the price of the brooms he had taken. Roisin could not believe her luck. Once again, she had sold all her wares, and the best part of the day was still before her.

She gathered up her few belongings and set off across the market square towards Coronation Lane and the palace. As she had the previous week, she marveled at the buildings and how they became statelier, their gardens more cared for, the closer they were to Coronation Lane. She came upon the little shrine of St. Dymphna and it surprised her at how far back from the road it was. Looking past it at the high stone wall, she felt a thrill of excitement as it brought to mind the adventure of the previous week.

While Roisin was making her way towards the gates of the palace, Emmaline was squirming in her chair in the tutorial room listening without hearing as her tutor related one of the countless historical anecdotes of which he was so fond. At the best of times, Emmaline, who never thought ill of anyone, found him to be pompous and a tedious bore and though a most patient student, today she could hardly wait to get out of that chair and down the stairs to the garden. Even the tutor, rapt as he was with the sound of his own voice could detect Emmaline's uncharacteristic behavior. "Your Highness, you seem to have a case of the fidgets today. Do you need to take a recess?"

Emmaline felt guilty about misleading him, but said, "Yes sir, I really do."

"Very well." he replied, then glancing at the clock added, to Emmaline's great delight, "It is getting rather close to the end of the day. Why don't we stop here?"

Not daring to risk a change of mind, Emmaline thanked him and was out the door before he could add another word. He paused a moment, amazed at the unaccustomed speed she had moved. Shaking his head in wonderment at the young of the species and their incomprehensible ways, he turned back to his books and his self-congratulations at another incisive and learned discourse.

Emmaline skipped happily down the corridor towards the glassed walled audience room. That was not characteristic of Princess Emmaline and any member of the court would be surprised seeing such girlish behavior and perhaps even worried by it. She was able to make it to the large windows of the audience room with no one seeing her. Once there, however, the crowds below spotted her. Most smiled and waved. Many bowed and curtsied. Whatever means they chose to honor their princess, all eyes were on her.

She was oblivious of all this as she scanned the faces of the crowd for Roisin. Once, she thought she saw her and waved. That resulted in a collective sigh that rose from the many admirers, most of who felt sure that the wave was especially for them. Fortunately, they couldn't make out the look of disappointment that followed as Emmaline realized that she had made a mistake.

She stood a long time searching through the crowd, but there was no sign of the person she sought. She stepped back from the windows drawing an unheeded round of applause from the many well-wishers in the garden. Emmaline's cheerfulness faded to gloom. She was more disappointed by the possibility that her newfound friend would not appear than even she suspected. For the next while, she wandered through the hallways, returning to the audience room windows from time to time to search the crowd again.

While the moments dragged on for Emmaline, for Roisin, the traffic on Coronation Lane seemed to be crawling. Despite the many walkers and shoppers that crowded the sidewalk, she still found it hard to control her urge to run. As it was, she trudged along with the throngs, from time to time, craning her neck to see any sign of the palace gates ahead. When she first caught sight of the ornate archways in the far distance, it was like a shipwreck victim catching the first sight of land. A surge of joy passed through her body like a shock.

She attached herself to a group of people who seemed to know each other and stayed close to them as they made their way up to and through the gates. As she passed the steely-eyed guardsmen, she felt a moment of panic again. Just as on the previous week, the guardsmen remained immobile, their rifles, bayonets fixed, framing the entrance to the palace grounds.

Once inside the palace grounds, Roisin took the first opportunity to slip away from the crowd. From a vantage point near the neat rows of tributes brought by many of the visitors to the palace, she scanned the grounds for anyone familiar. The only ones who were not guests where the young men in the brown and gold livery of the royal household. They were the ones who accepted the gifts of artifacts from the visitors, marked the information in a large leather-bound ledger and then took them to add to the already extensive rows of accumulated tributes

As she walked among the rows admiring the many treasures, she couldn't help but sense a growing tension. In the distance, the crowd before the audience balcony was slowly thinning. She knew she would have to find a secure hiding spot before very many of the visitors left the grounds, or she would be too noticeable to those still present. Then there would be no hiding, and she would have to leave with those who still remained when the trumpet blast signaled the closing of the gates.

She found a spot where the shrubbery grew more extensively, their branches forming a thick mesh against the grey stone backdrop of the palace wall. After making sure that no one was nearby who might be watching, Roisin wrapped herself in her dark grey blanket and curled herself around the trunk of one of the larger shrubs. There she lay, scrunched up in a tight ball, waiting for the trumpet blast signaling the closing of the palace grounds to visitors.

To Roisin, it seemed she had been lying there forever waiting for the trumpet to sound. As she waited, she fell into a reverie. Images and colors slipped across her imagination, but nothing remained long enough to make an impression. When the trumpet blast came, it startled her back to full wakefulness. Now she waited as the minutes crawled by. She tried to imagine the visitors leaving the grounds. There would be stragglers so it would take some time before the grounds were clear and the gates closed.

Allowing as much time to pass, as her tattered patience would allow, Roisin straightened herself out and sat up. Her heart stopped, and she almost shouted with surprise as a soldier, sword drawn, walked by so close to her hiding place she could have reached out and touched him. She froze where she was, knowing full well that if she followed her instinct to duck down again, he would hear her. She could only hope he wouldn't look over and notice her.

That the guardsman, as with his fellows the week before, passed by without seeing, or even suspecting the presence of the girl from the north country should not considered a failing. He was one of a corps of elite soldiers celebrated as representing the highest ideals of efficiency, effectiveness, and professionalism. The security sweep of the palace gardens after the closing of the gates was more for tradition than security as there had been no threat uttered against the palace or the royal family in memory. So it was, he continued his prescribed patrol and returned to report to his sergeant without ever knowing he had passed within arm's reach of an intruder.

Roisin followed him out of the corner of her eye until he was out of sight before daring to release her breath. As she gasped to replenish the air in her lungs, she rose awkwardly to her feet. Pressing close to the grey stone walls of the palace, the grey blanket still around her shoulders, she eased her way back to the rows of tributes.

Inside the palace, Emmaline saw the great gates close. As the guards made their security inspection of the gardens, she watched them, wondering if one of the guards might at any moment reach into some dark recess and come out with a peasant girl in tow. Although she was pleased that the guardsmen returned to their quarters without finding any concealed straggler, she was also worried that perhaps Rosie was not found was because she was not really there she hadn't come back.

With the guards out of sight, she was down the stairs and out the door. Micha, who had just come down the hall, could not believe either the speed or the gracelessness of her flight. That was Emmaline like he had never before seen her. Following behind with only slightly less reckless abandon than Emmaline, Micha revealed that he too was anxious to meet their secret visitor again.

Emmaline, racing as fast as she could through the palace grounds while Roisin, edging her way along close to the protection of the palace walls, saw each other at the same moment. Their faces lit up with joy and relief. Roisin forgot her caution and ran towards Emmaline. Princess and peasant, their usual reserve cast aside, embraced as if they were the oldest and dearest of friends. When Micha came up to join them, Roisin reached an arm out and drew him close. Micha was not displeased by this and joined in the embrace.

As the sunny warmth of the afternoon slipped away into the cool calmness of early dusk, the three friends enjoyed each other's company. Emmaline and Roisin, walking arm in arm, chatted animatedly. Micha was the consummate show off as he clowned and teased, strutted and pranced, glorying in the effusive laughter his antics drew from the two girls. On the previous week, a bond was formed between Roisin and Emmaline, on this week they cemented their friendship. The sense of friendship was so strong, so intense, it engulfed Micha as well.

When the single explosion of cannon fire signaled evening, the three friends met it with a resigned sense of disappointment. There was no panic on Roisin's part, just a reluctance to say goodbye to her friends. In the golden glow of the slowly disappearing sun, the three friends shared the certainty that they would be together again the next week and again and again for as many weeks as they could imagine.

They made earnest heartfelt farewells. Emmaline hugged her new found dearest friend Roisin. The flight from the guards to the secret exit was as furious as it had been the previous week, but for both Roisin and Micha, it was as much for fun as it was fear of discovery.

The nondescript peasant girl who slipped unnoticed from behind the Shrine of St. Dymphna to join the few pedestrians on Palisades Road had undergone a subtle change that day. If someone were to analyze her movement along the street, they would have noticed a confidence and purposefulness in her step out of keeping with the faded patchwork look of her clothing.

She reached the marketplace just as old Arram was harnessing up Jezebel. Sauntering up to them, she scratched the donkey behind the ears. Her eyes met Arram's, but she could detect no overt interest or curiosity about where she had been. He nodded a greeting which she returned as she helped him tie down his wagon cover. No words were spoken as he climbed aboard the wagon and except for a curt, "Gee up, Jezebel!" and a click of his tongue, that's the way it remained until they reached the bend in the road where their ways parted.

"Goodbye, 'Jezzie. See you next week, Arram," she said softly, giving Jezebel one more scratch behind the ear.

"Aye-ah," replied the old man, touching a gnarled finger to his forehead and nodding.

With that, he and Jezebel were off on their way, and Roisin was off on hers.

Once home, Roisin went about her daily chores with a new sense of purposefulness. Although neither commented upon it, both Ned and his wife noticed this and puzzled over it. If they were asked to express their feelings about this new Roisin, they would be hard-pressed to put words to them.

Emmaline, too, had changed. As with Roisin, it was subtle, and only those close to her would have any sense of it. She, like Roisin, appeared more confident, more contented and purposeful. It was as if the surrounding air was more energized. It was not something one could see in her behavior, but it was, rather, in her bearing. The only one to comment aloud was King Rafael, himself, who one day mentioned in passing to his wife that, "Emmaline seems to be feeling better."

If someone had been conspiring to have Roisin and her two friends from the palace spend time together, they couldn't have done better. The elegant lady who had bought Roisin's remaining stock of brooms that market day was King Rafael's cousin Duchess Elspeth. Her flair for design was famous throughout the kingdom. For the wealthy ladies, the height of fashion was to imitate Duchess Elspeth, in her style of gown, her style of shoes, her current coiffe. The upper classes and the wealthy considered her estate to be the avant-garde of interior design. So, when word trickled down to the gentry, the status seekers and social climbers about the Duchess' cunning incorporation of some unique handmade brooms into her household decor, handmade brooms became the height of popularity.

That these brooms were only found in small numbers at one of the lesser marketplaces on lower Palisades Road, was news more slow to spread. Still, it was enough to assure that all the brooms would be snapped up no sooner than Roisin laid them out for display. It was a tribute to Duchess Elspeth's power as a fashion leader that week after week, Roisin's wares were gone and her purse full before many of her neighbors in the market square had finished setting up.

Not only was Roisin able to be off for the palace gardens early in the day, but also with the approach of fall, the gates were scheduled to close at an earlier hour. King Rafael felt it was important that his children spend time in the gardens while the sun still shone. He ordered the tutors to shorten their lesson times so that the children could take advantage of the revised schedule.

The three friends had more time to share. They explored the palace grounds and investigated the long vacated sections of the old palace. While the adventurous Micha led them on escapades through the palace grounds, Emmaline and Roisin talked and laughed and bared their souls to each other. It was a happy time for the three of them. Micha had companions ready and willing to go adventuring with him, Emmaline and Roisin shared a fellowship that neither had dreamed possible.

The furious rush to the bolt hole to avoid detection by the evening guard became a well-timed, but casual departure. For Roisin, St. Dymphna was as familiar as an old friend. Palisades Road and Coronation Lane held no more awe for her. Old Arram and Jezebel still joined her on the quiet morning and evening journeys from the marketplace to where their pathways parted. There was no sense of curiosity or censure on the old man's part and before long the uncomfortable feeling she ought to explain to him how she spent her days vanished.

10

X. Secret Society

After having spent so much time together, exploring the old castle grounds and hiding from the guards, Micha decided that they had become a secret society. He wasn't sure what that meant, but it seemed to make sense to him that the label was appropriate. They were keeping their meetings and their adventures secret from everyone but themselves.

When he told the girls about his idea, they thought it would be fun. Micha suggested they call themselves the "Secret Adventurers" and the name was agreed on.

"We need some kind of secret sign, so we recognize each other. That is what secret societies do," suggested Micha.

The girls realized that they were only a group of three and already knew each other and didn't need secret signs. They also knew Micha was trying to add some more adventure to their visits and it would make him happy to have a secret sign, so they agreed that they should have something that would identify them as members of the "Secret Adventurers."

They spent a few minutes trying to come up with a one. "A

handshake isn't good enough," said Micha, "We need to have something we can see so we can recognize our members from a distance."

"Yes, "said Emmaline, "with a smile, "if Rosie was down with the crowds at the gate when we do our morning run with Papa and Mama up in the tower we could recognize each other and wave."

"For sure, " said Micha. "I have an idea. I'll show you next time.

True to his word, on the next visit together, Micha presented each of the girls with a gold-colored piece of twine to which he had attached a collar stud bearing a stamped engraving of King Rafael and the words, "Rafael XIV, Monarch" on a brass background.

Micha, who had explored inside the palace as much as he did outside, had found a large box containing these collar studs. They had accumulated over the years of Raphael's monarchy for every time there was some event of State over which Raphael was to preside, he was provided with two or three new sets of collar studs, one of which he would wear, and the rest his courtiers dropped into a large box. State events, while not constant, were frequent enough that the box was full.

Micha assumed that no one would miss three collar studs and he was right about that. What he didn't realize was their uniqueness. They were exclusive to King Raphael and found only in the royal chambers. The tokens the members of the Secret Adventurers were wearing tied them all to the palace. While Emmaline and Micha could wear the collar studs unnoticed by the surrounding courtiers, anyone looking at Roisin's token, anyone in the service of the monarchy or aware of court life, would wonder how a poor peasant girl could have gotten a hold of such a thing. Roisin encountered few of these people in the tiny, back-wall market where she sold her wares, and those she did paid little heed to the youthful broom seller.

In a little made up a ceremony, the three friends each placed the strings over the others head so that the collar button dangled down in front, glinting in the fading rays of the sun. There was something about these necklaces that made them feel special. Both Roisin and Emmaline each gave Micha a big hug and told him he was brilliant.

Micha beamed, and the friendship of the Secret Adventurers grew stronger than ever.

Roisin left the castle grounds that night feeling euphoric. The necklace with its shiny brass collar stud swayed back and forth as she trotted past the large statue of St Dymphna and onto the pathway that would bring her to the marketplace where she would gather her things for the long hike back home. She had never felt such joy.

The Secret Adventurers became as close a group of explorers and friends that one could find anywhere. Micha found in Roisin, whom he knew as Rosie, a fit and able companion who shared his high energy and love of exploration.

While ready for almost anything that Micha could throw at her, Roisin was sure to include the frail Emmaline she knew as Emma. If the going got rough, she would remind Micha that his sister was not as strong as he and he should be more considerate. Although Emma grew in strength from their adventures, she would never match the physical vigor of Micha or Roisin.

For Emma, as for Roisin, the best part of the weekly encounters was the intimate friendship they now shared. Despite their closeness, Emma had no idea of the impoverished conditions from which Roisin hailed, and Roisin was unaware her dear friend was none other than the well-loved princess of the realm, daughter of the great King Rafael.

They met on equal terms, both children of loving and caring parents encountering the transitions that would soon bring them to adulthood.

What Roisin did not realize was that she was no longer a peasant girl of little interest to anyone. She had become far more than just the peasant girl who sold handmade brooms in the small market near the back wall of the ancient part of the castle. She was no longer just a peasant girl who spent most of her life in the sere, arid and unregarded north.

Although she did not know it, she was now the close, in fact, the sole companion and playmate of the prince and princess. While this relationship, was, mostly, a secret to everyone, it still marked her as special, and the special relationship she shared with royalty would not go unnoticed while men like Duke Leonis' eyes in the city were around. Also, the marketplace where she sold her brooms was, as a place selling rare antiques and unusual items not found anywhere else. Because of that it became a favorite haunt of the wealthy and those of the nobility who thought themselves treasure hunters and enjoyed searching through the many unconventional items one could find only in this backwater market.

11

XI. Examining the Wall

As the days passed, Duke Leonis' agents in the North Reaches did their best to spread the seeds of discord, while Karl poured over ancient and modern blueprints of the palace, walked the public lands, and visited the many small markets that seemed to hug the palace walls. Sometimes he walked alone, but when he went to the markets especially the novelty markets behind the castle, he would bring his wife and her servants.

This would allow him to wander the market area, a patient husband, waiting for his wife to check out every curio and objet d'art that she could find in the market and to make her purchases. It gave him both time and freedom to examine the palace wall for any flaw that might suggest a hidden entrance. This was where ancient and hidden defense escape doors would be in locations near the oldest part of the castle palisades

On this day, Karl had brought his wife and her servants to one of the smaller and lesser-known markets at the far northern end of the palace. Treasure hunters, antique hunters and those who lived on the borderline of the North Reach were the attendees of this market.

Karl knew the back walls of the palace's gigantic and ever extending keep were ancient and thick. These walls had stood firm and, even without a moat to protect them, they had withstood many sieges over the centuries.

Still, every public place along the walls might conceal a secret exit or entrance, so well designed that one inspection, no matter how thorough, would never be enough in most cases. Several inspections would be required to be certain no exit or entrance existed.

Although this market square was one of the smallest in the city, it was near the back wall and close to the ancient north tower and the oldest parts of the palace. He had walked it after Leonis' command to him to find some way in, but it was a small market, and he was afraid his repeated presence might attract unnecessary attention. To distract or appease any eyes that had been on him, he decided that this would be one of those times he would bring his wife.

While she was shopping, he would play the role of the bored husband and be able to pace the walls. That would give him time to take a longer and more careful investigation of the part that lay hidden behind the garish flags and shabby barrows and kiosks of this out of the way market. His wife was beyond delighted to go with him crowing that this was the market where Duchess Elspeth had found all her exquisite artistic home furnishings such as those divine, handcrafted brooms she had purchased for next to nothing.

Upon reaching the market, Karl left his wife to examine the walls again. She was happy to spend some time among the barrows and kiosks and all those "adorable crafty and antique items."

Knowing Karl's dislike of shopping and his incessant puttering around the palace walls, she suggested that he meet her in about half an hour on the other side of the market where the young, red-haired country girl was selling her beautiful handmade brooms. Karl agreed. This meant less time he had to spend accompanying his wife, a slow shopper who gushed and cooed over almost everything she came across at the stands and barrows. Instead, he would have plenty of time to avoid the stalls and walk the length of the wall behind them. He could make a careful inspection before having to meet her where that girl sold those funny looking brooms.

Karl could not understand why anyone would buy something like that when there were far better made and more serviceable brooms to be had in the high markets at the front of the palace. He was practical man devoid of any artistic sense.

Having examined the wall to no more avail than the last time, he sauntered over to the small piece of ground space where Roisin spread out her wares. Even from across the square, he could tell that his wife was divesting the young lady of all her brooms. He walked up and stood just behind his very pleased wife, who, on his arrival, turned to Karl, gushing with delight, "Oh, the others will be so jealous, I've got the last of them.

Karl could tell. One of his wife's servants was loaded down with several handmade brooms and a large basket filled with silly things that his wife so loved and for which he had so little use.

"I will have more next week," said Roisin as she took the money from a second servant.

He stood by while his wife blathered on with the servants. When out of the corner of his eye, he caught the glint of shiny metal. It was attached to a string and hanging around the broom girl's neck. There was something about it. Modulating his voice to a tone that would make his words sound uninterested, he commented to Roisin: "That's quite an interesting little charm you have around your neck.

"Oh," said Roisin, placing her hand on it, "some friends gave it to me."

Karl wasn't sure, but it looked very much like one of those collar studs the King wore on state occasions, the ones with the state emblem and his name and title etched on the surface.

He would have liked a closer look, but his wife was now ready to leave. He would have to confirm if it was a royal collar stud another time. Despite his uncertainty about the shiny charm the girl wore on a string necklace, he felt confident it was information that would interest Duke Leonis.

12

XIII. If She Has Any Secrets

"Certainly," agreed the Grand Duke Leonis, "That is very interesting. If your supposition is correct, and it is one of Rafael's collar studs, there is no way that girl could have found it. If, as she says, she got it from friends, they are friends who live in the palace and live close enough to the royal suites to get their hands on the king's personal property."

"Yes, follow up Karl," said Leonis, "but be circumspect. We do not wish to alarm her as she would disappear back into the northern wasteland, or tell her friends whoever they might be, and that could cause us a whole other set of problems.

I know that Arve would just grab her by the neck and beat the information out of her, but we don't know how much or how little she knows and I suspect it is less than more. Check to see if it is a royal collar stud she wears and have someone keep an eye on her but from a distance. If she has any secrets, we'll dig them out, secretly."

"Highness," said Karl, bowing his head and departing.

Sometime later, Karl, Duke Leonis' trusted lieutenant was back in the market were Roisin sold her wares. This time his goal was to confirm that the token on the string around Roisin's neck was, as he suspected, an engraved royal collar stud would only be found in the palace, and exclusive to the royal suites.

He bought a few items from some barrows feigning inattention, he walked past the section of the market where Roisin was selling her brooms. Making it seem almost as an afterthought, he stopped and turned back to Roisin. "I believe." he said to her in a soft, pleasant voice, "that you are the one who sold my wife those delightful brooms. I must tell you she is thrilled with them; she tells me they are of exquisite construction. May I have a look?"

As Roisin bent to pick up one of the last of her brooms, the customer bent down too. Roisin stepped back, startled. "Oh, I'm sorry," said Karl, and he backed away from her.

He had achieved his goal. It was one of King Rafael's collar studs she had on the string around her neck.

He could see she was agitated, to calm her down, he feigned interest in the 'exquisite construction' of the broom and offered Roisin two coins. "I'll take it," he said.

The amount surprised Roisin: "Oh, that's too much. I don't think I can make change for you."

"Oh," returned Leonis' agent, "Think nothing of it. They make my wife so happy, and we've always felt it was important to support our nation's craftsmen. Use it well," he added as he smiled and turned away.

Had anyone been watching, they would have seen old Arram's eyes coolly follow the Duke's Lieutenant as he sauntered across the square. Once beyond the market, Karl tossed the broom into the bushes, near the Parkette of St. Dymphna "I can't believe I said those things; 'delightful broom, exquisite construction,'" he muttered and laughed.

His laugh cut off, Karl strode off without so much as a sidelong glance at the Grotto of St. Dymphna and the many statues that stood near it.

Karl reported that it was indeed one of the king's collar studs to Grand Duke Leonis, who leaned back in his chair looking at his entwined fingers. He looked up, "and she is being watched?"

Karl confirmed that with a nod. "Good," said Leonis, "now let's sit back, relax and see what secrets get spilled."

While one of Karl's observers tracked Roisin to the palace gates and watched her enter and waited for her to leave, another stood in a small stand of trees that offered him both concealment and an unobstructed view of the market and the approach to it. There were others in other locations, but this was the one who saw Roisin making her way to the market as the first fingers of dusk were reaching out to cover the palace wall in shadows.

When the watchers told their stories to Karl, he realized that although the girl was going through the front door to the palace, she was leaving by a back door. The following market day determined to discover where this back door out of the palace was, Karl set out his watchers. They covered every bit of the wall with their surveillance. Roisin could not leave the palace grounds without one of them seeing her.

Despite their careful watch, they saw no door, but one of them saw Roisin appear as if from out of nowhere in St. Dymphna's parkette.

They set up watch again the next week with the focus on the parkette and once again, the girl appeared as if from nowhere beside the huge statue of the saint.

13

XIII. St. Dymphna's Parkette

"St. Dymphna's Parkette," said Leonis, more to himself than to Karl and the watcher who had seen Roisin's magical appearance in the park.

"Yes, interesting," continued Leonis, "the wall takes an unusual jog there. What an excellent spot for a bolt hole or raid window behind that ancient grotto."

In the old days when the palace was a castle, and the world was more warlike, there would be secret escape doors or bolt holes built into the walls through which the Royal family could get clear, should an invading army laying siege get too close for comfort. Other secret exits allowed loyal troops to sneak out of the castle and carry out raids against forces holding the castle under siege or to establish a second front behind the enemy. Since the castle had given way to the palace, most of these were more likely to be found in the ancient parts of the old castle, now neglected and in ruins and any knowledge of such bolt holes and raid windows was long forgotten.

Karl and his watchers dressed in dark colors, blackened their faces to make them invisible to any passers-by. They set up their watch on the shadowy edges of St. Dymphna's Parkette. Roisin who had stayed a little later than usual did not see them as she stepped out from the grotto and around from behind the statue. She jogged toward the market to gather her things. then make her way towards home along the dusty path beside the muddy rivulet that had once been a large, life-giving river.

As soon as Roisin was out of sight, Karl and his men made their way to the grotto. In the fading daylight, they could see nothing despite their absolute certainty that an exit from the palace was there somewhere. They lit lanterns and used the light to see if they could detect any sign of a door. They found none. Perhaps, they hoped, in the full light of day it might just reveal itself.

The next day, disguised as park maintenance workers they examined every millimeter of the rough and crumbling stone of the ancient grotto, but the stone refused to reveal its secret. They could find no hint of a doorway or passage. This was a well-designed bolt hole, perhaps the best ever made by the craftsmen of the ancient kings. Even if Karl's men were to trace the outline of the door, it mattered little, for these bolt holes were set to never be opened from outside the castle. It was a true one-way door. Should one have pushed the exiting Roisin aside and grabbed at the door to hold it open, it would be of no use. Safety mechanisms would hold off even a squad of men and continue to close the door taking a few fingers with it if need be.

Roisin or anyone else could leave and at will, but nothing, short of the battering of a heavy and wasteful cannonade would reveal any sign of the door and passage behind it. Even with the cannonade, traps that released brick and rubble to fill the passage only augmented the security of the bolt hole.

Karl brought the word to Leonis who was unhappy, but not surprised. His own castle in the West March had similar, well defended, escape portals.

"Do we take the girl and question her," asked Karl.

"To what end?" replied Leonis. "We know how she gets in, and we know of how she gets out, and I would wager that's about all she would know about the palace fortifications. That said," continued Leonis, "she is important. I think she might be the key, but to find that out, we must dangle her a little longer.

14

XIV. Caught

The weekly walk along the Palisades Road and up the broad and busy expanse of Coronation Lane became a familiar ritual for Roisin. She would stride up to the palace gates and under the bayonets of the stern-faced, unblinking guards. Despite her confidence, she never once passed by those two sets of eyes, their gaze focused on some far horizon, without feeling a pang of misgiving. She often wondered if they saw her, or indeed if they saw anyone among the constant flow of people in and out of the palace gates.

Had she but known! Her bouncing, confident step, her soft flaxen hair, free and shining, her bright-eyed face that showed the early signs of adult beauty had caught the eye of one of the younger guards, a certain Underlieutenant Matricht.

Each week, he would watch her enter the palace grounds and many things about her puzzled him. Her plain, almost ragged attire and itinerant's pack was so out of place with the usual finery of most visitors to the palace. This and the fact she came alone while others of her years came in the company of adults sparked his interest and curiosity. Having watched her enter the palace grounds so often, he watched for her leaving. At first, he felt he was missing her departure. The press of the exiting crowds at gate closing was large, and it was possible that in the crush she could leave without his noticing. Each week he searched the crowd with more care, his frozen expression hiding a growing sense of puzzlement.

He suspected she was not leaving the palace grounds with the others when visiting hours ended. he questioned his fellow members of the evening watch. They had seen no one in the gardens except the young prince and princess. The morning guard detail had no memory of young girl dressed in peasant rags leaving the palace grounds during their gate duty.

The young guardsman was now facing a full-fledged mystery. A ragged adolescent girl went through the gates into the palace grounds each afternoon of market day and then vanishes.

The guardsman did not know how long this had been going on. As a loyal officer in the elite Royal Guard, he knew even with no other consequence, this was a very serious matter. This mysterious young girl, it seemed, was eluding the kingdoms' best trained and efficient soldiers, soldiers whose lives were dedicated to protecting the king and his family. Whether this girl was a threat to the king and his family or not, she was a threat to the image and good name of the Corps of the Royal Guards. He brought the mystery to his superiors who, although they remained skeptical of his conclusion, ordered that he bring her in for questioning the next time she shows up.

So, it was on the very next market day, Roisin was to discover that her feelings of misgiving each time she passed by the guards at the palace gates were a justified foreshadowing of doom. Her approach to the gates was now so familiar that her thoughts and her attention were on the upcoming encounter with her two friends. When, like thunder breaking around her, came the crisp, shouted command, "Halt."

It failed for an immeasurable moment to register with her. Then the barking command, the sudden barrier of a rifle barrel and bayonet awoke her to a shock of terror unlike any she had ever experienced. Gripped with fear she could not move. Her eyes focused on the glistening blade of the bayonet, didn't see the awed crowd move away from the gate. She heard but did not see the guardsman as he shouted for the sergeant of the guard and then her mind went blank.

Roisin understood little of the immediate proceedings. She saw the tall man in the white with the black trim uniform crimson sash and saber of the Royal Guard, standing before her. There was a crisp exchange between him and the guard who held her at bay with his rifle. She didn't see a third guardsman step into place at the palace gates but heard the command from the man with the crimson sash to come with him. And although she could not see him, she felt a sensation of white heat on her back from the weapon held menacingly in the hands of the guardsman who marched behind her.

Inside the guardhouse, she found the soldiers to be polite. Although far from being put at ease, they gave her a moment to absorb what had happened. From his place, seated behind a desk before which Roisin was told to stand, the duty sergeant questioned her in a polished and precise tone. She told him who she was and where she came from. Although he seemed to share the national blind spot for the northern part of the kingdom, he wrote it down.

Having gone through the preliminary questioning, he then asked Roisin her business at the palace. Roisin was sure that her two comrades inside the castle might be in serious trouble if she told the truth. To protect her friends, Roisin made up the story which could be true in a country that adored its monarchy. The story she told was of a sickly grandmother, so fascinated by the Royal Family she had sent her granddaughter to gather as much information as she could about them. When the sergeant asked her about her regular visits, she embellished the story saying that the grandmother wanted to know every detail of the palace, its grounds and anything she could see of the royal family itself.

When the sergeant asked her why she was often seen entering the grounds but was never seen leaving, it caught her by surprise. Unable to think of anything else, she blurted out she might have fallen asleep under the bushes, as she was often exhausted from her long journey from the north. She had heard from Emma that they opened the gates in the early hours of the morning to let staff leave to shop for the kitchens and to allow nonresident serving staff to enter. She told the sergeant she was able to sneak out then.

This seemed to satisfy the sergeant. He closed his file and rose to his full height. "Miss, you are forbidden to enter the palace grounds again. Should you do so, my guards are under orders to detain you as a prisoner of the crown until you are returned to your parents. Do you understand?"

Roisin nodded weakly in response. "Good," said the sergeant, turning towards the young guardsman, "escort her to the gate."

As he led the shaking, ashen-faced girl towards the gate, it surprised Underlieutenant Matricht to discover that he felt bad for her. He had an urge to console her, but he felt that to do so would be area breach of duty and of discipline. He marched her to the gated entrance to the palace grounds. In front of the curious gaze of the many entering the palace grounds, in a crisp, unmodulated military voice, he charged Roisin to leave the palace grounds and not to return under pain of detention. He watched with intensity as she left.

No words could define Roisin's feelings. She felt so lost and saddened as she walked down Coronation Lane. Her shoulders sagged. She focused her eyes on the ground in front of her as if to hide the humiliation she felt.

When she got to the Shrine of St. Dymphna, she could restrain her pent-up emotions no longer and burst into tears. The awful realization struck her she would never see her dear friend Emma again. The adventures with Mitch were over. Stumbling over to the statue, she slumped to her knees, buried her head in her hands and cried bitter tears. A most precious part of her life was gone. It was as if all feeling had been drained from her body. When she could gather herself back together, she rose to her feet, turned her back on the shrine and the palace walls beyond and began the long journey home.

From that moment on, her life became rote. This sudden change from Roisin's usual cheerfulness worried her parents. They suspected the weekly journeys to the city might be coming too much for her. They assumed that Roisin was finding the trip arduous and unrewarding,

Roisin was unable to explain it was the distance, but the emptiness she felt at being separated from her friends. She felt at the end of it. It was very difficult for her to return to the Palisades Market, to be so near yet so far from her dearest friend, Emma. And yet, when her parents asked if she wished to give up the trip to market each week, Roisin refused. She so wanted one more chance to get inside the palace to say a last goodbye to Emma.

On more than one occasion she would set out towards

the palace with great resolve, but one look at the cold-eyed guardsmen flanking the gates and the resolve would fail. She tried the escape route behind the Shrine of St. Dymphna, but the stone would not budge.

15

XV. The Girl is Gone

Often Underlieutenant Matricht would see her in the distance, a forlorn figure among the milling throngs. She seemed so different from the bright-eyed, happy girl who had attracted his attention with her light-hearted, bouncing step. It troubled him to see her like that. This confused him. He couldn't understand why he felt that way. She was just a peasant girl of no consequence, and he had done his duty in reporting her to the Sergeant of the Guard. Yet, even across the distance, she kept from the gates, he could see a terrible sense of loss and he felt responsible.

Matricht wondered just what it was he had taken from this girl. He could not help but think it was something important. He became so obsessed by a need to find out what it was. It took all his inner strength and loyalty not to leave his post and rush over to her.

In his off-duty hours, he would wander the streets in the poorer parts of the city hoping he might encounter her. Not only did he not find her, but he could find found no one who looked as poor as the red-haired girl dressed in her tattered and patched clothing. It was as if she vanished off the face of the earth only to reappear before the palace gates again the next week. Underlieutenant Matricht gave up trying to find her around the city. Whenever he caught sight of her, he would try to dismiss her from his thoughts. There were more immediate concerns to take his attention.

Karl could sense it. There had been some kind of change. The girl had stopped going to the palace although she remained in the market to sell her brooms and then returned north when the market closed. While she still showed up at the market, she never got closer to the palace than the little food stands a respectable distance from the gates. Leonis was not happy about this development.

His plans to follow her, to learn more about her time inside the palace gates from Karl's informants inside, to find in her some leverage that might move his treasonous plans forward, were foiled. He would have to find another way. Oh, how he cursed the young bucks of the Guard for turning her away from the gates and complicated things for him.

16

·

XVI. A Turn for the Worse

A pall had fallen over the palace. Princess Emmaline's health, always frail, was failing. King Rafael and Queen Alyssa were beside themselves. They sought the best physicians from around the world to come and examine her. None could find a cause for her decline. She seemed to waste away. There was nothing left to do but make her as comfortable as possible. The palace gates closed earlier in the day so her ladies and the nurses could bring Emmaline into the garden to catch the last warm rays of the afternoon sun.

His superiors gave Underlieutenant Matricht a citation in recognition of his careful attention to duty while standing guard. The Corps prided itself on its ability to attend to the minutest detail, and the Underlieutenant's report regarding the young peasant girl had caught the eye of his superiors. As a reward for his dedication at the gate, they decided to remove him from gate duty and assign him to the palace Life Guards.

As a member of the palace Life Guards, one of his chief duties was to provide escort for Princess Emmaline throughout her daily stint in the palace gardens. Like the rest of the population, his concern was with the weakening princess. He thought no more about the peasant girl at the gate.

Each day, he would greet the princess and her nurses at the patio entrance and lead her wheeled pallet down the cobbled path to where the day's tributes were gathered. There, he would watch the princess as she stared wistfully at the array of trinkets and treasures.

At first, he, like all the others at the court, thought Emmaline had chosen the spot because the sight of all the tributes was soothing to her. It seemed as if they sparked something in her spirit. Underlieutenant Matricht had seen it himself. A

At first sight of the tributes; the Princess would raise herself up to look around. He couldn't miss the eagerness in her eyes, nor could he miss how fast it faded to a dull indifference. He soon recognized that the tributes meant little to Princess Emmaline. He could see that any interest she showed in any of the curios and trinkets the nurses brought her from the piles was feigned. He was impressed by the consideration, the ailing princess showed the nurses as they fussed over her like mother hens.

As the days passed, Princess Emmaline became less and less attentive to her nurses. The spark of interest her eyes revealed at the first sight of the tributes grew increasingly fleeting. The Underlieutenant found it very difficult to watch his princess. He was certain she was dying and yet he felt that there must be some way to save her. When commissioned as a member of Princess Emmaline's personal Life Guard, he had pledged his life to protect the princess. He took it as a matter of dedication to duty and personal pride to do all he could to help her.

Although he felt that something about the collected tributes was important to Princess Emmaline, he suspected it was not the tributes themselves. When at her side, he would gaze around the grounds trying to find in their surroundings something that might suggest to him what Princess Emmaline sought there. He could find nothing that might offer the slightest clue. He feared there was no hope, and he was destined to watch the Princess continue to fade.

The days continued to pass. Princess Emmaline slipped into delirium where she would carry on conversations with the air. The nurses would gather around trying to understand what she was saying, but now she was seldom articulate enough to be understood. They could catch some phrases. The ones she repeated over and over "Where are you, Rosie?"

"Oh, there you are, Rosie, come over here, I've missed you."

Hearing this, the nurses thought she was looking for Roses. Since no roses grew in the garden that time of year, they ordered a bouquet of red roses from a local importer. Eager with hopeful anticipation, they handed her the roses. To their dismay, she gave them one glance and dropped them. She looked off into the distance and reached out her arms as if to grasp someone. Her voice was faint as she spoke, "Come on, Rosie, take my hand, we'll walk through the gardens. I've so much to tell you. Oh, Rosie. Where have you been."

She made as if to rise from her pallet, then fell back in a swoon. The frantic nurses were convinced that the roses had had some mysterious effect on the Princess. As they swarmed around her trying their best to make her more comfortable, they prattled on about the roses. "Perhaps we should get white roses!" exclaimed one.

Another cut in to suggest they order a variety of colors. Another suggested that it might be rose bushes the Princess wanted. "Alive and growing in the garden." added the first.

Underlieutenant Matricht wanted nothing more than to tell the nurses to just get lost somewhere where they could carry on their irritating chatter out of his hearing. He needed to think, and he needed quiet to do it. "Ladies," he said in his most diplomatic tone, "perhaps we should let her Highness rest and enjoy the last bit of warmth from the sun."

Their words stopped short. They nodded their agreement and in silence took up their station around the pallet. The princess seemed to be resting easier. Her breathing was relaxed and steady. She appeared so tiny and frail to the Underlieutenant. Her skin was pale and fragile looking like fine parchment. It was difficult for him to see her so wasted. He could neither look away nor could he forget her weak distant voice calling out to, "Rosie." Who or what was this Rosie? Underlieutenant Matricht had to find out. He was certain that "Rosie" did not refer to flowers. Perhaps it sounded more like a name.

At debriefing that evening, he asked his captain if there was anyone named Rosie at the court. The captain thought a moment then shook his head. He had been with the Life Guards for many years and never; he told the Underlieutenant, had he ever heard such a name. "If there ever was a Rosie around the princess, then this Rosie would have to have dropped out of the sky."

The words, "dropped out of the sky" thundered in the Underlieutenant's ears. Was that the answer to the puzzle? Perhaps Rosie was a small bird or animal that had somehow endeared itself to the princess. Someone as solitary and gentle as the princess might well have befriended some tiny creature. Now, in her delirium, she wanted it for whatever comfort it might bring her. Underlieutenant Matricht had difficulty sleeping that night. He was sure he was on to something.

17

XVII. The Search is On

With the morning call to muster, the Underlieutenant's mind was racing. He had to test his theory. While the others hurried to the mess hall for breakfast, he headed out the door and into the gardens. He poked among the bushes and the trees, trying desperately to keep his dignity and military bearing while calling out in a high piping voice, "Here Rosie, Come on Rosie."

He prayed that he would get some kind of result with his singular quest, but he could never have guessed how his prayer would be answered. Fanning through the shrubbery near the palace walls, he was emboldened by the emptiness of the garden to call louder for Rosie to come. He was so intent on his purpose that when a child's voice asked him, "Why are you calling for Rosie?" He was so startled that he almost fell over.

Seeking the source of the voice, he looked up to see a boy's face peering at him through a small palace window. recognizing the face, he stood to erect attention and snapped a salute, "Good morning, your highness. I hoped that I might find Rosie."

"Don't you know," said Prince Micha, with a sad shake of his head, "Rosie doesn't come around anymore."

Whatever this Rosie was, Underlieutenant Matricht could see that Prince Micha knew something. He felt he dared not let this drop. "Why doesn't Rosie come around anymore," he asked.

"I don't know," said the prince, "She came and came and then one week she didn't come back. She's not been around since, and we miss her."

"We?" asked the Underlieutenant.

"Me and Emma, we don't have any fun anymore. Now Emma's sick, and there's no Rosie to come and play." There was an inescapable sense of sadness in the young Prince's voice.

"Where did she go?" asked the Underlieutenant. He was grasping to make some sense of the Prince's words.

"She went out by the Satyr's Gate when the evening watch came on. Then she never came back."

The Underlieutenant knew of no Satyr's Gate anywhere around the Palace. "This Satyr's Gate, I've never heard of it."

"It was our secret," said the prince.

"A secret gate! How exciting!" Underlieutenant Matricht realized that he must be very careful about what he said at this point. "Where did it go?"

"Out into the city." replied the Prince matter-of-fact voice.

"Oh really!" returned the Underlieutenant using the most off-handed and disinterested tone he could muster without being insulting. Prince Micha had quite a reputation for mischief, and he could be stringing him along with his story of a gate.

"You don't have to believe me if you don't want to," shrugged the Prince.

"I didn't say I didn't believe you," countered the Underlieutenant. Matricht realized that he was close to losing the Prince.

"I'd just like to see it, that's all. You couldn't tell me where it was, could you?"

"Yes," said the Prince, "I could take you. It's not much fun now, anyway."

Visiting the secret exit again intrigued Micha. He also knew the Underlieutenant was honor-bound by years of training to protect him, even at the expense of his own life. The soldier seemed to know something about Rosie. And, he couldn't resist the opportunity to show off a little.

"Wait a moment," he called down to Underlieutenant Matricht and then disappeared from sight.

The Underlieutenant called after him, "But how will you get out to the grounds?"

"I have my ways," came a smug voice from close beside him.

Prince Micha stepped out from behind a bush, and Under- lieutenant Matricht could see in the young Prince's eyes he did have his ways. There was no doubt in the young guardsman's mind that Prince Micha would be someone to be reckoned with when he grew older. If it were possible, his sense of confidence in the future of the kingdom had increased dramatically, as he looked into the steady eyes of his diminutive companion. "His bodyguard will have his hands full," thought Underlieutenant Matricht to himself.

"O.K., Your Highness, let's see your Satyr's Gate."

At first he followed without a word as Prince Micha led him along a maze-like path. The benign neglect that marked the grounds and structures of the older sections of the palace intrigued him. Then, he had to ask the question. "Your Highness, who is Rosie?"

The Prince had realized that the guardsman knew little about Rosie. He might have thought it better left that way, but he was feeling some of the thrill and enthusiasm he had shared with Rosie as they raced to elude the evening watch. This made him feel generous towards his companion. "She was our friend, mine and Emma's. We played together a lot, but Emma and Rosie liked to talk. Emma was happy when Rosie was here, but now…."

His voice trailed off.

"What did Rosie look like," the Underlieutenant wanted to know.

"Rosie was a girl. She had freckles and red hair. She wore those funny clothes."

"Funny clothes?" asked the Underlieutenant.

"Yes, they were old and patched. It was as if they were all she had." His tone expressed his mystification at this possibility.

"They were all she had!" exclaimed the guardsman, his mind was working overtime.

Things were falling into place. The girl at the main gates was Rosie. Somehow, she had made friends with the Prince and Princess. She would come each week to visit with them and stayed until the gates closed. When Micha showed him the Satyr's Gate, just as he had promised, it all became clear to the Underlieutenant. Had he not noticed her at the gate and become curious, she might still be making her weekly visits. This girl was the Rosie that Princess Emmaline was calling for. The chilling realization dawned on him that he might have contributed to Princess Emmaline's tragic condition.

On the return from Satyr's Gate, Prince Micha, relaxed and invigorated by his sojourn with the guardsman, kept up a steady string of chatter. He told everything he knew about Rosie, which wasn't very much. He knew she came from somewhere around the Palisades Market and had to sell something there and that she had been surprised about how popular whatever it was she sold had become.

When he said goodbye, and disappeared behind the shrubs, the guardsman could not bring himself to follow him and see how he got into the palace. When the Prince appeared at the upper window to wave, Underlieutenant Matricht snapped a brisk salute which ended in a wave, Then the Prince, was gone from sight and the Underlieutenant was alone with his guilt.

That afternoon, standing watch over the almost lifeless Princess Emmaline, he resolved that he would undo the harm he had so unwittingly caused. He bent near to the princess and whispered in her ear. "Your Highness, I promise, as God is my witness, I will find your Rosie and I will bring her to you."

Princess Emmaline's eyelids fluttered, then opened to look at Underlieutenant Matricht. There was an awareness he hadn't seen for some time. Then, her eyes closed. She relaxed and drifted off into a deep sleep.

That evening, for the first time since his assignment to the palace, Underlieutenant Matricht asked for a short leave. If this surprised the duty officer, he showed no sign. He stamped a three-day pass and handed it over.

18

XVIII. Looking for a Girl

A short time later dressed in civilian clothes the young Guardsman was among the hedgerows of the palace gardens heading towards the older section of the palace. Twilight was fast approaching, and the pathway became harder to see as he hurried along. As he rounded a large Yew, he almost knocked over one of the evening's Watch. Both were startled. The guard of the Watch could utter his challenge in his surprise at finding someone in civilian dress so far from the front gates and the inhabited section of the palace. Recognizing the Underlieutenant, the guard of the Watch recovered his composure. "Oh, it's you Matricht. You gave me quite a start. We don't get many people here. What's up?"

The Underlieutenant gave an unbelievable story about having an interest in history and wanting a closer look at some ancient structures of the palace. "I see," said the guardsman, with an exaggerated nod, "Well, this time of evening is perfect for examining old structures. But," he added with a broad wink, "it's even better for examining young structures, perhaps female ones. Wouldn't you say? You never know when one of those off-duty nurses you're hanging around with all day might just stumble down one of those dusty corridors," His smile was smug, "to examine old structures, too, no doubt."

The guard stepped aside, to allow the Underlieutenant to continue down the pathway. As Matricht passed, the guard let out a low, unmilitary whistle, then turned away. This was perfect as far as the Underlieutenant was concerned. It was his luck to encounter the most single-minded "lady-hunter" in the corps.

Thanks to the lusty imagination of his fellow guard, he now had the perfect excuse for wandering around the palace grounds after sunset. He was well aware that before long, the rest of the evening watch, and the night watch, too, would have heard a well-embellished fantasy explaining to everyone's satisfaction where Underlieutenant Matricht was. He might have a few rough weeks of ribbing in the barracks, but for now, he was free to come and go without question.

The fading light cast an eerie glow about the burial chamber. In the silence, the Underlieutenant could hear his heart pounding. He would rather have been anywhere else at that moment. Inside the tomb, the darkness was stifling. He struck a match and with the tiny amount of light it cast, moved from image to image along the wall. By the time the third match sputtered and died, he reached the back wall. The fourth match's first burst of flame revealed the satyr's hollow eyes.

The match was still burning as he went through the passageway and moving the huge rock back from the exit. He marveled at how light it felt and how smooth it was sliding aside. It rolled back into place behind him. He took a moment to see if he could open it again, but to no avail. Its fashioner was an ingenious craftsman. Peeking around the statue of St. Dymphna, he could see that the street was clear.

Moments later, he was walking north along Palisades Road with no idea what he would do next. Rosie was out there somewhere, and somehow, he would find her. He paid little heed to the change in his surroundings as he walked.

Underlieutenant Matricht was busy trying to remember every detail of what Prince Micha had told him about this Rosie. He wished that he had been less preoccupied with his sense of guilt and had done a better job of listening. He also wished he was more attentive when the Sergeant of the Guard had interrogated the girl. He was not sure he was going the right way. He had no idea where he might find her. He continued on trusting to the intuition that had brought him this far

The last traces of daylight had disappeared as he entered the Palisades Market. Although he was aware that he could expect nothing more at this time of day, his heart sank at the sight of the deserted square. The sense of depression overwhelmed him as he looked about at the closed doorways and darkened windows. In one shadowy corner of the square, several empty barrows were shoved together as if huddling for protection against some hostile force. He had no idea what to do.

For the longest time, he stood, frozen in place, his mind blank. The faint sound of music and laughter coming from somewhere close by brought him back to awareness. Looking for the source of the sound, he saw it came from a public-house at the far end of the square. The faintest glimmer of hope stirred as he crossed the square towards the light and sound of the pub.

Opening the door, he could see a boisterous crowd gathered around the bar. The mood changed the moment he stepped into the room. All eyes were on the stranger. It was clear to everyone that despite his youth and casual attire, this stranger was a man with a position of authority. They looked away and resumed whatever it was they had been doing but now with an undertone of wariness that hadn't been there. The Underlieutenant recognized it. It would not be easy for him.

Putting his jacket on the coat rack, he walked over to stand against the bar. The pub keeper was busy drying a glass. He held it up to the light, eyeing it carefully. Whatever his investigation had discovered, he gave one last swipe to the glass then set it on the bar. With a deliberate motion, he faced Matricht as if noticing him for the first time. "What can I do for you, sir?" His tone was well modulated, neither too formal, nor too familiar.

The Underlieutenant asked for a tankard of dark ale. He leaned against the polished oak of the bar while the pub keeper pulled the drink and slid it over to him. Matricht tossed some coins on the bar, and the pub keeper swept them up and dropped them in the till. He watched the Underlieutenant from a discreet distance for several minutes and then moved up to him. "I haven't seen you around here before. What brings you to our part of town?"

"Well," thought the Underlieutenant, turning to face the barman, "direct and to the point."

He had a strong feeling that direct and to the point was the way to be here. "I'm looking for a girl."

"We're not that kind of pub," returned the barman in an even tone.

"It's not that kind of girl," Matricht's tone, too, was even.

The barman made no reply, but a look of puzzlement crossed his face fleetingly. "Oh," he said with polite interest, "who might this girl you seek be, then?"

The Underlieutenant had caught the fleeting look on the barman's face. He also noticed that the barman had raised his

95

voice for the benefit of those around. "I'm not all that sure," he replied, "I know that she is young, in her early teens, and dresses like a pauper. I've also been led to understand that she has a sales space at a market near Palisades Road. This is the first market square in this area I've seen."

"This girl in some kind of trouble?" asked the barman.

"Trouble?" said the Underlieutenant in a tone that attempted to convey to all who listened that this anything but the case. He gave his head an exaggerated shake so that the curious clientele would see it. "No, no, no trouble, no. I'm looking for her on behalf of a friend who needs to speak to her. No, no, anything but trouble."

"Well," said the barman, his voice lowering, "This is the only market out this way and tomorrow's market day. Who knows, lots of people set up shop around, you might just find her."

Underlieutenant Matricht nodded his thanks and turned around to study the lounge area. The barman returned to drying the glasses. As if on cue, his patrons began leaving. Passing the bar, most bid the barman good evening by name. They all nodded at the newcomer leaning against the bar. The Underlieutenant returned their nods. When all but a few patrons were gone, he turned back to the barkeeper. "Beg your pardon, sir, but could you tell me where I might find some lodgings for the night around here?"

The barkeeper set down his towel and with a sweep of his hand pointed to a set of stairs at the rear of the lounge area. "We have here as good accommodations for a night's rest as you're liable to find anywhere around. If you're not looking for something fancy, I could open a room for you."

The Underlieutenant expressed his satisfaction with that and tossed some more coins onto the bar.

The room was spartan but as comfortable as the guards' barracks. He walked over to the tiny window that looked out on the dark and deserted square below. He knew the market square would soon be crowded with the buyers and the sellers. Somewhere among the many merchants, there would be a young raggedy girl named Rosie or so he hoped. If she was there, it would be for him to find her. His short time in the pub clarified for him he would not get any help in his search, but he felt no opposition, and for this he was grateful.

With a deep sigh, he crossed to the bed and stretched out on it. As he lay there, it occurred to him with disturbing clarity that this whole venture depended on what Prince Micha had told him. Having only encountered the prince on the one occasion, he didn't know if he was given to flights of fancy. It did not help his confidence knowing all he had ever heard about the young prince was that he was always up to some mischief. As he drifted off into a restless sleep, he could only hope that the prince's apparent sincerity was genuine.

19

XIX. GlimpsingRosie

When he awoke, the morning sun was streaming through the window. He got to his feet. He had slept far longer than he had intended. Splashing water on his face, he crossed to the window and looked out.

The Market Square was already crowded. He rushed down the stairs and passed a startled housekeeper. She half jumped, half curtsied as he went by. "Damn," he muttered to himself as he threw open the pub door and stepped into the street, "Does everyone know I'm an officer in the guard."

Lady fortune that had brought him this far smiled on him again. This market was popular with curio hunters many of whom made their homes within the palace or in the mansions close by. Among the crowds, he wasn't worth more than a passing glance. At least he could wander unhindered among the many shoppers and merchants.

By noon, he had covered most of the market square. He was certain that there wasn't a square centimeter he had missed.

Heavy with despair, he stopped at a snack food kiosk for a spicy fruit drink and a buttered bun. This was the first he had eaten since early the previous day, and although it would have tasted wonderful after months of mess hall meals, he couldn't enjoy it. He slumped down on a nearby bench. What began so full of hope the night before was now near hopeless. He paid little attention the two well-dressed ladies who set down their bags of purchases to sit beside him. So, he was a bit embarrassed to find himself listening to their rambling conversation.

It was not an inspiring conversation court gossip interspersed with talk of millinery and designers and where to get the best fashions. As the two women chatted on, he was immobile. He wanted nothing more than to leave, but something held him there. It may have been his feeling of despair, or it may have been an agonized hope that somewhere in the tangled web of their conversation he might discover something that would help him.

When one lady smiled, and waved at someone in the distance, he glanced in the same direction. A woman of obvious wealth was leading several package-laden servants through the crowd. "Who was that?" asked one lady to the other.

"Oh," replied the first, "It was Lady Angela and her porters.

"Out looking for priceless objects d' art, no doubt." said the other.

"Well," returned the other, "Duchess Elspeth found those cunning handmade brooms here."

"Yes, yes Elsie and her brooms," the tone was not one of deep affection.

"If I recall," Stated the first lady, "you were quick to jump on that bandwagon, my dear."

"Well, yes, it's true. They were appealing, but that was months ago," responded the other sounding apologetic.

"You know," said the first, "I have a daughter who could use one of those brooms for her room."

"But, my dear," said the second lady, "they are so out of fashion."

"To tell the truth," laughed the first lady, "I wasn't thinking of decoration. Let's go. I wonder if the girl is still here."

Was this what he was looking for? Underlieutenant Matricht felt a stir of hope. He was up and following the two ladies at a discreet distance. Rounding the large barrow of a cloth merchant that was festooned with a striking and colorful display, the Underlieutenant almost walked right into the two women. His eyes went past them and fixed on the familiar features of the young girl from the gate. He could hardly contain his joy. He had found Rosie.

He had recognized Roisin right away, but she had seen him coming before he saw her. To the surprise of the two ladies, she let out a short gasp and the broom she was holding dropped at their feet. Then she was off between the barrows with the fleetness of a gazelle. Without hesitation, the Underlieutenant pushed past the two ladies almost sending them sprawling. He had no ear for their protests of indignation as he raced in desperation to catch the running girl. "Wait," he called, "don't run, I only want to talk to you."

Where the slender Roisin could slip with ease among the stalls, he could not. He must have bounced off five or six hard corners before he had to stop. The girl was gone.

He limped back to where Roisin had dropped her broom. He picked it up, looked it over, then set it back down. Oblivious of the crowds, he sat down on her stool and cursed the luck that had brought him so close to his goal only to leave him so far away. He knew she wouldn't be back and he couldn't blame her for running. Her only experience with Underlieutenant

Matricht and the palace guard must have been devastating to her. Given her circumstances, he felt he might have done the same.

"Wouldst not do harm to her, t'would not be wise." said a soft voice from close by.

Looking up, Underlieutenant Matricht saw the old man, Arram, standing over him. His clothing was the worse for wear, and his aged face was not much better. "Go away, old man", said Matricht his tone sullen, "I've no time to waste with you."

"Ayah, it 'pears to me lad thou hast a goodly bit o' time to spare an old man."

Peeved by the old man's insolence, Matricht was about to shoo him away in much stronger terms. He rose to his full height about to unleash on the poor old fellow all his pent-up frustration only to find himself speechless, riveted by the most intense pair of steely grey eyes he had ever seen.

"Young sir," said Arram, "If thee be seekin' harm to the young Lady Roisin, thee may find to thy dismay that thou'st chosen wrong girl."

Matricht wanted to laugh at the old man's threats, to tell him he was the one to make the wrong choice, but all he could say was, "I had no intention of harming her. I need her help."

"And now, young guardsman, thou needst my help." Old Arram pushed past the Underlieutenant to sit on Roisin's stool. "I'm an old man, now, and I treat better sittin'."

If Underlieutenant Matricht was amazed that his occupation neither surprised nor intimidated the old man, he was more amazed at himself. Within minutes, he was pouring out his story to this old stranger, confiding in him as if he had known him for years. Only then did he realize how heavy was the burden of guilt he carried. If he had not set out to show how clever and alert, how superb a guardsman he was, the Princess Emmaline would not be on the verge of death. He should have investigated more carefully. He should have learned how important this peasant girl was to the princess.

"Aye." said the old man, "'Tis a woeful tale to be sure."

The Underlieutenant looked into the piercing blue eyes, then looked back towards his feet. That was it. He had just bared his soul and all the response he got was, "'Tis a woeful tale."

The two sat together awash in silence for what seemed to be the longest time. Then, the old man stood up. He drew himself up to his full stature. It was quite an imposing figure that Underlieutenant Matricht looked up to when he raised his eyes. More imposing was the voice, crisp and clear and with no trace of a rustic accent. "This is no time to lose yourself in grief, soldier. You are an Underlieutenant of the Royal Guards. You have a duty to perform. Your country and your princess need you."

The tone brought Matricht to his feet. No master sergeant he had met in training could match it. "You will not find that girl here today. She's very frightened, and she's a smart one too. But, I can help you."

To Matricht's complete amazement… this was a day of surprises…, the old man explained how he could trace the girl to her home in the north.

He felt invigorated and excited once again. He trusted the old man. Why he should, he wasn't sure, but he did. In an act of spontaneous gratitude, He took the old man's hand surprised at the firmness of the grip, he looked straight into the steely blue eyes. "Remember, soldier," said the old man, "I'm not doing this for you, I'm doing it for the princess, and for the young Roisin. Treat her with gentleness and care."

"I will, I will," promised Matricht as he gathered up Roisin's belongings she left scattered on the ground.

As he left the market, he turned back to catch a brief glimpse of old Arram as he disappeared into the crowd. Once again he was a bent and feeble old man. It was hard to believe the old peasant was the same person who had called him to attention just moments earlier.

XX. Mysterious North

Back at the palace, Matricht ignored the snickering of his off-duty fellows as he made his way through the barracks to the stables. Saddling up his black charger, he was through the gates and on his way back to the market. From there, he headed towards the crossroads near the merchants' church where a narrow path turned northward. Soon he had left the city behind.

As he rode, the landscape became increasingly depressing. The lush trees that grew near the city gave way to gnarled and bent bushes. He found it difficult to believe such a desolate and lifeless land could be a part of the kingdom. Why had he never heard of this? His country had always been portrayed as a land of plenty; the seaports and factories of the south, the mineral-rich mountains, and forests of the west, the verdant, fertile plains of the east. But, what of the north? And it occurred to him he had never heard much of the north part of the country.

He could recall no mention of it in his history and geography classes at school. No recruits from the north had shared barracks with him at basic training. For the first time, he recognized that the north country was a blank to him as if it didn't exist, yet here he was, less than a day's ride from the city, passing through a vast expanse of bleak and gloomy countryside. It was hard to reconcile this with the image of the beautiful and prosperous nation he carried in his mind.

All the long afternoon and evening, he rode the dusty pathway stopping only once to feed his horse beside the filthy brown trickle that meandered sluggishly through the grey dirt and strewn rocks of the dry river bed.

21

XXI. Sad and Alone

Lost among the streets of the city, Roisin wandered directionless keeping close to the shadows while glancing back over her shoulders watching for pursuers. She was terrified and heartbroken. She could not understand why the guardsman was chasing her. Perhaps she had come too close to the palace on one of her sad visits to the front of the Palace. She felt she had lost everything.

She knew she could now neither return to the marketplace to retrieve her belongings nor take her place among the merchants there ever again. She must have done something terrible.

Realizing that evening was falling, there was little left for her but to make her way home. How would she face her family and tell them that she could no longer return to the city? Her parents were honest folk and loyal to the king. What it was caused the guardsman to pursue her, it must be very serious. She couldn't help but feel that somehow she had brought shame upon her beloved parents. With these thoughts burdening down her heart, she began her slow trek homewards.

She was able to orient herself with the help of the dark aspect of the north tower and was on her way up the dusty path into the North Reaches and home. As devastated as she had been, unable to visit her friends Mitch and Emma in the palace, this feeling was different. She felt she was a wanted criminal, a fugitive. Home no longer seemed a safe refuge and the entire city was forbidden to her. When she stopped along the way to rest, she had no blanket, no copse of trees for warmth. She found a smooth place among the bare rocks and did her best to sleep.

It was a fitful and restless sleep she awoke from as the first fingers of light reached above the eastern horizon. The morning came in clear and frosty, and she bundled her ragged clothing around her as best she could to stave off its icy bite. Lost in her sense of despair, she allowed her step to slow matching her feeling of impending doom.

When she came over the hill and saw her home, it looked so cheery with the smoke billowing from the chimney and the light reflecting off its pale stones. Tears welled up in her eyes. As she approached the front door, she was so lost in her anguish she failed to notice the sleek black stallion munching grass beside the stable door. If she had, she might have been more prepared for what was to happen next.

As it was, she pushed open the door to find her mother busy at the stove. She turned and flashing a relieved smile ran to Roisin. "Darling, you're home. Thank goodness. We were so worried. Are you all right?"

Roisin nodded her head wearily. "Sit, dear," said her mother, "I'll get you breakfast. And, there's a gentleman to see you."

Out of the corner of her eye, Roisin saw a familiar figure rise from a chair beside the kitchen table. Panic overwhelmed her. In desperation, she looked around for an escape, but there was nowhere to run. She stood trembling as Underlieutenant Matricht crossed the floor to stand before her. Roisin's legs were so weak that she was unable to stand. Seated at the table, she made herself as small as she could. Her terror was palpable to the young guard.

Underlieutenant Matricht sensing her panic and recognizing the in her eyes and stopped. "No, no, miss," he blurted, "I am not here to harm you. I'm here because I need your help."

Roisin felt some reassurance in his tone although she didn't seem to understand his words. She began to cry. "What did I do wrong? What did I do wrong?" she asked between the sobs.

"You did nothing wrong." Shaken by Roisin's tears, the Underlieutenant reached out with a tentative touch to her shoulder.

Roisin's mother came to the rescue. "Come, dear, sit down. The Underlieutenant has something important to tell you," she said and led her to a chair.

The Underlieutenant, a look of sympathy on his face, pulled up a chair and sat facing a very confused Roisin.

"Do you know of a girl named Emma who lives in the palace?"

"Yes," stammered Roisin, "But I haven't seen her since you told me not to."

"I Know," said the Underlieutenant, "I've seen you in the square outside the gates."

"Did I break the law being there?" Roisin's voice was a strained squeak.

"No, of course not," said the guardsman. "You have done nothing wrong. I'm here because a friend of yours needs you very much."

"A friend?" asked an incredulous Roisin.

"Your friend, Emma, is sick. She has been asking for you."

"Emma!" Roisin sat up eyes wide with concern. "She's sick?"

"She may die," said the Underlieutenant trying to squeeze from his mind the thought she might be dead already.

Roisin's gaze was one of concern as she watched the young guardsman and said nothing.

"She has been calling for someone named Rosie. That's you, isn't it Roisin?"

Roisin nodded her head. "She very much needs you, Roisin. Will you come back with me to the city and visit with her for a while?" begged the Underlieutenant.

There was a moment of silence as Roisin's mind sought to understand all she had just heard. Then in a voice so strong and determined that it even surprised her, she responded: "I would do anything for Emma," and she was on her feet ready to go.

Not long after, the guardsman astride his charger with Roisin holding on for dear life behind, were off down the road towards the city. It astonished Roisin how much faster they traveled on the horse. She could tell they were getting close to the city when the Underlieutenant reined the horse to a halt so it could eat and rest. Roisin's mother had packed a lunch for them to take along which she shyly offered to the guardsman. Sitting down on some rocks, they both ate in silence, watching the horse searching out a snack among the tiny weather beaten shoots along the edge of the road.

"I'm sorry I've caused you so much trouble," said Roisin, her voice soft and restrained.

Underlieutenant Matricht hung his head at her words. "No, Roisin, it is I who am sorry for causing you so much trouble."

Looking directly at him for the first time, Roisin could see the sorrow etched on his expression. It puzzled her. "How have you caused me trouble?"

"I deprived you of your friends."

"But I wanted to spend time with my friends so much that I hid in the palace grounds and didn't leave when the gate closed. I could have frightened or offended the young prince or princess. I had no right to be there."

Matricht looked up at her disbelieving. Was it possible she didn't know? "You never frightened them, Roisin; you don't offend your friends by spending time with them."

Roisin's response was a look of misunderstanding. "Don't you know, Roisin? Princess Emmaline calls out for her best friend, and it is you she names. The rest of us honor your Emma as our princess, the daughter of our sovereign lord. You honor her as her friend, and in her moment of need, it's you she calls for, you, her dear friend, Rosie."

She heard, but couldn't comprehend. "I... I don't understand."

"Don't you get it yet, Roisin, the boy, and girl you befriended in the palace grounds were Prince Micha and Princess Emmaline."

There was wonderment in Roisin's voice as she repeated to herself, "Emma is Princess Emmaline, and Mitch is Prince Micha."

It was beyond belief and yet as she thought about it, it made sense. There were never other young people or children in the palace gardens, just the three of them. The gates were closed, and the grounds searched before they came out. How was it she never once suspected the possibility?

In her mind's eye, she could see Emma and Mitch. In that vision, there was no doubt of their identities. As she entertained that idea, she realized that she felt no awe. Emmaline and Micha were special friends. They were not special because of their rank and position, but because their friendship was special.

110

Princess Emmaline meant far more to her because she was Emma, another person with whom she shared a special bond. Now, her closest, truest friend was sick and needed her. She must get to her as fast as she could.

As if he read her mind, the young guardsman was already in the saddle and reaching his hand to help Roisin up behind him. They were once more off down the dusty path towards the city.

22

XXII. Where Have You Been?

Near the city, snow had started falling from the puffy, cotton ball clouds scattered against the blue backdrop of the sky. In the bright, afternoon sun, it was like countless priceless jewels wafting in the light breeze. The flakes appeared as glistening silver stars against the midnight black of Underlieutenant Matricht's horse then faded and were gone.

Everything had a surreal, almost mystical appearance through the curtain of gleaming, fluffy snowflakes. Neither Roisin nor the young guardsman could appreciate the spectacular beauty of the surroundings. Their thoughts were on a dying girl, each in their own way praying they wouldn't be too late, that somehow they could help.

Then they were out of the trees. The city loomed before them, the dark face of the North Tower softened by the falling snow that swirled around it. Soon the horse's hooves were clattering on the cobblestone streets as they followed the twisting, turning roadways among the shops and homes. The two riders were oblivious to the curious stares of pedestrians.

Many stopped to watch the tall young man on the king's horse and the ragged waif of a girl holding on behind as they rode past. Along the crowded Coronation Way, they rode towards the palace gates with the same single-minded focus on their destination that had carried them through the barren pathways of the North Reaches. The people on the street must have sensed the urgency of the riders' mission as they stepped, without complaint, out of the way

Reining in his horse in front of the closed gates of the castle, Underlieutenant Matricht called out in a loud, and imperious voice, "Underlieutenant Matricht at the gates, seeking entry on the king's business."

The guards at the gates shouldered their rifles and in one voice called out, "Sergeant of the Guard, Sergeant of the Guard. A friend seeks entry on the king's business. How say you?"

What seemed to Matricht and Roisin to be forever, but was in fact only a scant few moments, the gates clanked open. Passing through, Underlieutenant Matricht snapped a salute and called out to the bewildered Sergeant of the Guard as he galloped past. "I'll get back to you with a full report."

Seeing one of the Princess's attendants, he reined to a sudden halt and called to her, "Where's the Princess?"

The attendant, startled by the sudden and unexpected appearance of the riders tried to respond but was, for the moment tongue-tied. She waved her arm in the general direction of the garden. Horse and riders were off before she could offer a garbled, "In the garden, by the wall."

Nurses and attendants flew in all directions as Matricht urged the horse through the garden, into the glass-roofed gazebo and right up to the pallet on which the emaciated form of the princess lay. In what appeared to be a single motion, he had leaped from the saddle and lifted Roisin to the ground.

Roisin raced to the pallet. She could not hold back the gasp that slipped from her lips as she looked at the pale, pinched face of her friend. She took Emma's hand in hers and was amazed at the delicate dried parchment feel. Roisin bent down on her knees beside the sleeping form and spoke to her. "Emma, Emma, it's me, Rosie. Please, speak to me, Emma."

It seemed to take forever before there was a response. Then, the Princess Emmaline's eyelids flickered, and she looked at Roisin. "Oh," she said in a faint, fragile voice, "Rosie, it's you."

Those who watched could not believe what happened next. Princess Emmaline lifted herself up on her elbows and twisted to face Roisin. In a tone showing a level of awareness no one had heard from the Princess in many weeks, she said, "Rosie, it is you."

It was as if a heavy weight had fallen from her as she repeated, "Rosie, it is, it is you. You've come. I knew you would."

"How could I not come?" asked Roisin, her voice shaking with tears.

"Oh how I've missed you, Rosie,"

There was a stunned silence among the Princess' attendants as they watched their princess reach out her arms to hug the patched and ragged peasant girl. "Never stay away like that again, Rosie. Don't ever."

"I won't, I promise," whispered Roisin.

"I need to rest, now, Rosie," said the Princess. "Sit with me for a while and then; perhaps we will have lunch together. There is so much to talk about."

Roisin helped Emmaline to lie back on the pallet. Their eyes met, and both smiled. Then Emmaline closed her eyes.

Those who had seen it swore that a miracle had taken place

as the soft snow fell in that garden. With the peasant girl beside her, Princess Emmaline was resting, as she had not done for months. Before their amazed eyes, color came back in her face. There was a new vitality to her features. For the longest time, no one moved for fear they might break some magic spell. No one moved except for Underlieutenant Matricht, who realized that something wonderful had happened here and the king and queen should know about it.

By the time the Underlieutenant was back with King Rafael and Queen Alyssa, the princess was sitting up talking animatedly to her friend. The Queen broke into tears and ran to Emmaline's side. They shared a warm embrace while King Rafael stood over them, a huge smile on his face and an equally huge handkerchief in his hand with which he seemed to be blowing his nose. Seeing him, Princess Emmaline reached her hand out to him and pulled him closer. Roisin could only stare, wide-eyed. This was the king and queen.

After several moments, the king and queen turned to face Roisin. Roisin froze, as much in disbelief as in fear. "Mommy, daddy," said Emmaline, "I want you to meet my very best friend in the whole wide world. Her name is Rosie. Rosie, this is my mommy and daddy."

An awed Roisin could only nod. Then in a most unregal move, Queen Alyssa stepped over to the peasant girl and hugged her. "Thank you for giving me back my daughter,"

King Rafael squeezed Roisin's hand and smiled down at her. "My daughter's very best friend in the entire world, I am for ever grateful. You are most welcome here."

Just then Prince Micha came running into the Gazebo. "Rosie," he shouted, "We found you. I knew we would. How are you? Can you stay?" and he grabbed her free hand.

"Well," said the king giving his son a fond look, then back to Roisin. "I must say, young lady, you come well regarded by the younger members of my family. I have always found them to have impeccable judgment…," he looked back at Micha, "at least in the matter of friendship and the sort, perhaps not always in matters of behavior," and he gave Roisin a big wink.

"Now, you must have lots to talk about as I understand from Underlieutenant Matricht that you haven't seen each other for quite some time. It is so much warmer inside why don't we all go in and talk over a cup of tea?"

23

XXIII. Homesick

The next few days passed for Roisin as if in a dream. The palace was wonderful. Emmaline was making a rapid return to health. When she was awake, Roisin spent every moment with her. Micha wanted his time as well and soon games of "Hide and Seek," " Follow the Leader," and tag seemed to be breaking out everywhere in the palace.

Roisin's kind and generous nature made her an instant hit with the working staff. The king and queen were as good as their word. They were welcoming, and kind and treated her like a member of the family. Everything was wonderful, but she missed her own family.

In the first excitement, Roisin had little time to think much about them, but as the royal household routines returned to normal, she found she missed her mother and father very much.

One evening Queen Alyssa encountered Roisin seated in front of a large window that overlooked the palace gardens. In the fading twilight, the city with the lights all lit seemed a sparkling, many-faceted jewel against the dark border of countryside and sea. Roisin sat with her elbows resting on her knees and held her head in her hands. Although she rose and beamed a broad smile, the moment she was aware of the queen's presence, it was evident to the queen that something was amiss. "What is the problem, dear?" she asked her voice both gentle and solicitous.

Although Roisin claimed all was well, Queen Alyssa could see that this was not the case. She persisted in her questioning until Roisin confessed how much she missed her family. Queen Alyssa was dismayed and horrified to think it had never once crossed her mind that Roisin might have a family she would miss. She felt it was a heartless oversight on her part and determined to set things right. Rushing to Roisin's side, she put her arm around her shoulder, "Oh, Roisin, dear, forgive us. We have been so thoughtless. You have given us so much, and we have thought so little about you."

"Oh, no, Your Majesty, that's not true." exclaimed Roisin, "you have been wonderful. You have showered me with kindness."

"We must get you back to your family right away, Roisin." said the queen.

"Please, please, Your Majesty, the Princess is not well yet. I can't leave her."

"Well," said the Queen, "We will do something. I shall speak with Rafael," and she left the room.

A short while later, to his great surprise, a call came for Underlieutenant Matricht to go to the palace. The king wished to see him. Hurrying through the great wooden doors of one of the secondary audience rooms, the young guardsman almost ran into a pacing, King Rafael. The distracted King waved off his flustered salute. "Underlieutenant," said the king, "I must confess to a very serious oversight on our part."

A quizzical, "Sire?" was all he could respond.

"Yes, and I feel I am the most heartless buffoon in all the

kingdom."

Underlieutenant Matricht's expression could not conceal his utter puzzlement. "You have no children, do you Matricht?" asked the King.

Without waiting for a response, he continued, "No, of course, you don't."

The speechless Underlieutenant could only shake his head to show that that was the case."

"Well," continued the king without hesitation, "I do, and if there is one thing I cherish beyond all else, it's my children. I love my children." The king, pausing, peered at the guardsman

"Yes, Your Majesty, of course." Matricht nodded his head in agreement.

Turning away, the King went on, "If someone rode off with one of them, I would miss that one terribly, don't you see?"

Taking a deep breath, the Underlieutenant interjected, "I'm not sure I understand, Your Majesty."

The effect of that seemed to stop the king cold. He paused for a moment then pointed to a chair. "Please, sit down."

Matricht sat down and watched dumbfounded as the king pulled up a chair and sat down to face him. "The young lady, Roisin… we have been very thoughtless. We forgot that she is just a child and has a family of her own. I'm sure they must miss her. Wouldn't you say so?"

It occurred to the Underlieutenant that this was true. His brief encounter with Roisin's parents had impressed him with their deep love for their daughter. "Yes, Your Majesty, I would."

"Indeed," said the king, "… and Roisin misses them. She will not leave Emmaline's side until she is well. She has said so much herself. So, we must bring her family here."

This was something that the Underlieutenant could deal

with. "Sire, I will set out this minute to extend Your Majesty's command to the Norick family."

"No, no, no," said the king, rising to his feet, "not a command, an invitation and from me, in person. It's only a matter of common courtesy. I would like you to join me first thing in the morning and bring me to their home so I myself, might escort them back here. Will you do that?"

"Sire." Matricht intoned his ready affirmation as he rose to his feet snapping off a brisk salute.

"Then it's settled." The king turned to leave, then stopped and turned back again, "Please join us for breakfast. It's served at eight, right after I take my exercise."

With that, the king went through a small door at the back of the chamber. Underlieutenant Matricht watched the door swing shut behind him. He stood there transfixed for several moments, then in his best military manner, saluted the closed door and was on his way back to the barracks at a brisk trot. It was a bemused young man that entered those barracks. He did his best not to think about it, but an invitation to dine with the king was not something given or taken lightly.

He had just opened his footlocker to check on the condition of his dress uniform when one of the queen's pages appeared at his side. "Her Majesty wishes you to know breakfast will be informal and that you should dress informally."

24

XXIV. The Ambush is Set

"The peasant girl was found, and the princess is healing. Rafael has the Genealogists tracking down the girl's ancestry," Karl reported.

"Always the stuffed-shirt, that Rafael," joked Leonis, who was far more concerned about heritage and status than Rafael could ever be."

"To be sure, highness," Karl agreed, then continued with his report. "There is talk that the king may ride out himself to request her parents join their daughter at the palace. Plans aren't finalized, but some think the whole family will take the trip to the North Reaches.

"Keep me posted, Karl." Instructed Leonis, "If the king is planning to ride to the north, it might give us our opening. Dates, Karl, times… find out."

Karl bowed and was about to leave. Leonis stopped him with another instruction, "Call in the men for a meeting at my castle this evening, Karl."

Karl bowed once again and was off to carry out his assigned duties.

Left alone, Leonis slipped into a reverie he was having more often, and he was now certain this dream was about to become a reality. He could almost see the king and his queen jogging the tower stairway to the observation deck and back twenty-five times in a row. "After your jog," said Leonis out loud to no one in particular as no one was there, "you will be fit... fit to yield your crown, to me. I will end the mindless rule of the hawk, the family Aspitair, the family 'dead duck' will be your new title as your line that has mired us in this damned mediocrity fades into history. The Leaping Leopard of the family Leonis will bring order and strength back to this country. Our neighbors will tremble before our roar."

He couldn't resist rubbing his hands together and stamping his steel-clad heels on the massive table. "Perhaps we will meet on the path to the north, eh, Rafael," crowed the Grand Duke.

The Foresters were gathering. They had left behind their many essential duties. Such important duties left behind included such things as spying and sewing discord, collecting fines, and beating up any poor poacher. Never mind that most of the poachers were most likely frustrated farmers who dared to rid their farms of one of the plentiful deer or boars that came from the borders of the Grand Duke's personal playground, the woodlands of the West March, to trample their fields and despoil their gardens. This happening after many petitions to the Duke for assistance.

Assembling at Leonis' beloved Winter Court in the Castle Leonis of the West March the Foresters crowded into the large room, milling about and talking until Arve entered. Arve was more loyal to Leonis than any of the others were. He had been a Captain in the Rangers, a career officer who had lost his rank and post when the last vestiges of the force had disbanded. He was offered a choice of posting with the Guards, or with the Navy but refused them both. He was not going to be a tin soldier in the Kings household, or stand on the deck of some old tub to take the salute of some doddering old admiral. He knew if Leonis was king, he would restore the Rangers to their ancient glory and there would be a role for him

What Arve had kept from his days with the Rangers was a military bearing and a commanding voice that could bring the Foresters to order. "Gentlemen," he commanded, "to order, please, his Highness, the Grand Duke Leonis of the West March and battle chief of the nation wishes to speak to you."

A wave of silence swept over the room as the Foresters, following Arve's gesture, turned towards the entrance through which, Duke Leonis would make his formal entrance.

Embedded in their silence was the certain belief that this was not the general run-of-the-mill meeting. They were aware that some important decisions that would affect them were made. And, from this moment on, their roles, the Duke's role, and the nation would change forever. Anticipation filled the air.

Entering the room, Leonis saluted the men, who returned his salute. He was wearing the dress Kepi of the Rangers on his head and the camouflage dress tunic of an officer of the Berserkers. Many of his followers were moved by this, as many of them had worn the dress Kepi, or the camouflage tunic as members of the Rangers or Berserkers. Two regiments, now extinct symbols of the nation's militaristic past.

Although none had known the glory days, they all despised the inglorious disbanding of even the Ceremonial remnants of these two proud fighting forces.

Karl's messengers had bypassed old Sir Stanley when the Foresters were called to the West March. He and his wife were holding a card tournament at their stately home, and Sir Stanley was the busy host.

Had Sir Stanley heard Leonis, it would have horrified him as this talk was callous treason. As loyal as he was to the Duke, Sir Stanley was just as loyal to the king.

"Gentlemen," said Leonis, "sometime in the next two or three days, our silly king and perhaps, some of his family will ride into the North Reaches tomorrow. The roads there are poor, ill kept, and narrow. The king and his retinue will be on horseback. Don't let his honor guard fool you; they may be Royal Guardsmen, but those riding with him will be the elite.

I say this because this is might be our one chance to bring this effete monarchy to an end and restore our nation's former glory.

We will set an ambush where the North High Road turns left at the banks of what remains of the Grande River of the North and runs between it and the slate hills.

Arve will command. He will assign you your duties. At this very moment, weapons are being drawn from the secret arms cache at the Horn River Redoubt.

Arve has told me," continued Leonis, "that despite the efforts of his team, the people of the North Reach, while unhappy with the neglect, still respect and support the king. In ancient times, they were the king's strongest supporters. It was Northerners who formed the Guard. They have an ancient loyalty to the present monarchy, and it will take some time to overcome. There is no help for us there, so this mission you are about to embark on must be a secret one. Not the slightest hint of our plans can get out."

Gesturing towards Arve, Leonis offered another revelation that showed his confidence in the correctness and expected success of his plan. He named Arve to be the first brigadier of the restored Rangers because as far as Leonis was concerned, victory was assured. And the power to restore the disbanded fighting forces was his.

Leonis would leave it to Arve to assign the Foresters their battle roles and to distribute the weapons when they arrived. Having done this, Leonis rose to his feet to leave, "I leave you now," he said, "but we will meet soon on the slate hills. where the Great North pathway turns left along the muddy trickle of the Grande. Our moment of victory is at hand."

The Grand Duke Leonis left the castle in the certainty that his perception of justice would be served and within days, he would be king of the land. His hubris would brook no thought of failure. In his mind, he and his men were braver, fiercer, better trained and smarter than the King's so-called skilled Guardsmen, and his advisors. There was enough truth in this to admit the possibility of success, only Leonis' blind hubris turned possible to certain."

"Hail Duke Leonis, Hail King Leonis," The men shouted as he exited the hall.

Leonis had to admit to himself that hearing his men calling him King Leonis did make him feel good. His loyal Foresters had left but the gloating smile still burned on his face.

25

XXV. Important Business

Arram, as was his routine, in the early hours of the first day of the week, drove his cart pulled by the loyal Jezebel to the old clay pits just beyond the slate hills. Digging with his small shovel, he would fill a barrel with this superb potting clay. Northern ceramics had once been famous for their strength and beauty, but that was back when the laden barges from the ceramic plant, now only ruins beside a stagnating stream, would twice a day make the journey to the city along the mighty Grande River.

The barrel of clay loaded onto the donkey cart, Arram would sit on a large stone bench, a crumbling symbol of better times, and puff on his pipe. He might contemplate the history of the area or the events unfolding in the city with the Royal family and the potential usurper, Duke Leonis. While he sat, the patient Jezebel picked through the dried grass for any sweet green stems she could find. Then he would return to the city following the narrow path by the muddy river bed. A path that once, long ago, was a broad highway beside a mighty river that coursed through a prosperous land.

To any observer, this elderly rustic engrossed in his thoughts and focused on his journey he was unaware of anything else. That observer, however, would be wrong. Arram was nowhere near as old or self-absorbed as he appeared. He had an acute awareness of his surroundings and little escaped his subtle surveillance.

By the time he had passed the slate hills on his way back towards his home near the city, Arram had discovered a good many things. He knew armed men were gathering atop the slate hills. Recognizing, faint though they were, some more prominent voices, he knew they were Leonis' men, members of his so-called Foresters. These men, he knew, were up to no good. He also knew sooner than later, King Rafael, some of his staff, young Prince Micha and a handpicked squadron of his Guards would ride North to find the man he called, Ned o' Reaches They would follow the same path Arram was now on. The path would bring them to the foot of those slate hills where Leonis men waited. He also knew it was no coincidence those armed men were up on those hills.

Arram's view of The Grand Duke Leonis was colored by disdain. This disdain was toward a person so arrogant and so self-serving he would push a young rider and her horse off a cliff to their deaths. As a young man, Leonis was uncaring and unconcerned about the consequence because he was in a hurry and he could not bother to slow down till she got by him. Despite the disdain for the Duke and the ever-present pain of the loss of his niece, Arram had long since eschewed violence.

His understanding of the Grand Duke, however, was clear and precise. Leonis loved to wield his power and hungered for more. He wanted to be king so he could revive the militaristic traditions of the nation's distant past. It was a time of war and conquest.

War and conquest were what Leonis craved, and he was, as he demonstrated those many years ago, ready to push anyone aside who might stand in his way.

King Rafael along with his son and heir were soon to ride into Arve's trap. With them out of his way, Leonis would fall heir to the throne. What better place than the forgotten north to carry out the brutal assassination of the king and natural heir?

They would lay the blame for such a regicide at the feet of those rebellious northerners. A few northern rebels' violent reaction to the historical neglect and poverty in which the monarchy had left them. Anyone with any knowledge of conditions in the North would never question the truth of this allegation. It would provide a new monarch, King Leonis, a perfect opportunity to demonstrate to all his strict approach to justice.

Arram was well aware of the character of Duke Leonis. He knew when the ambush occurred, Leonis would not take part. He would, however, stay very close so he could strut like a rooster in front of the fallen King. Arram knew, too, that Leonis' treachery must fail. This was not only about Arram's deep loyalty to the king and his family, and his love of country. It was also personal.

"Come Jezzie; let's make time," urged Arram, "we have some important business in the city."

26

XXVI. The Colonel Returns

Arram's destination was the Royal Guard Barracks in the older part of the city, and Jezzie had made excellent time. Like her master, Jezzie was younger and faster than she appeared. It was no bent old man that stepped down from the donkey cart, but a tall straight and somewhat imperious figure exuding confidence and command.

Although the young man at the gatehouse had seen the elderly gentlemen ride up on his donkey cart, he hadn't noticed a change in the old man's bearing. He could only see the rustic clothing and while wary as a guard needs to be, what he was not prepared for was the sharp tone of command that issued from him: "call the duty sergeant, private."

Taken aback by the tone that came at him with the terrifying familiarity of a drill sergeant's order, the young guard, without hesitation, called out: "Sergeant of the Guard, to the gate."

An older man, not as imposing as the guard, dressed in the less formal fatigues, the working man's uniform, a three-stripe chevron on his collar, looked out the barrack's main door. Seeing the roughly attired civilian, he walked to the guard box.

Ignoring Arram, he turned to the young guard whose stance had stiffened ever so little: "What seems to be the issue, guardsman,"

"The person at the gate requested I call you, Sergeant," came the crisp response of the guardsman.

He did, did he," returned the sergeant, "and did he say why he wanted the Duty Sergeant?"

"No sir," replied the young guard.

"Did you ask?" continued the sergeant.

"No sir."

"Don't you think you should have done just that before opting to waste your sergeant's valuable time.

Although the young guardsman was certain that the sergeant's valuable time was already being wasted on a game of solitaire, he made a professional response, "Yes sir."

Still ignoring Arram, the sergeant went on, "Perhaps when some raggedy old person comes to the gate and tells you to call your duty sergeant, you should clarify with that person why you should disturb your…"

Tiring of the sergeant's obnoxious harang of the young guardsman, Arram, in the same tone of command used with the young guardsman, spoke up. "I asked him to call you because it is your job to ask the questions and the guard of the gate's job to remain alert and vigilant and refer visitors with questions to the Duty Sergeant."

That had gotten the sergeant's attention turning his anger away from the young guard and onto Arram. "And who are you to say what my duties are?" We are not here to commiserate with the rabble…"

"Don't you think you should find out why I asked for you," asked Arram, ignoring the sergeant's tone.

"I don't care…," began the sergeant.

"I wish to speak with Major Jaekman.

"Oh you do, do you!" said the sergeant, "that can be arranged," he added as he called out, "Watch. To the gate."

Four men in combat dress bolted out through the barrack's door and rushed to the gate, "Sir?" asked the first to arrive.

"This bumpkin wishes to see the major," stated the sergeant, "Take him in."

The sergeant's meaning was clear to the four members of the Watch. They opened the gates, one going to each side of Arram and taking him by his arms. With two walking close behind, the soldiers holding Arram's arms steered him in through the gates and in the door of the Barrack's public reception area.

It was all so familiar to Arram. Dark wood wainscoting rose halfway to the ceiling and a light amber colored stucco completed the walls; several doors opened on to small rooms each furnished the same, two chairs facing each other over a simple dark wood table. Two or three other chairs stood against the wall signs on the door labeled them, "Interview Room," each having its own number starting with 'One'. It was close to a gated wooden barrier behind which was a large desk with the sign Duty Sergeant and the name of the particular sergeant who enjoyed that role on that day.

Benches lined the walls, and several old leather chairs occupied the open space. Four chairs were placed around a table that held some cups and spread arrays of playing cards in front of each chair. Above the duty sergeant's desk was a huge clock that ticked ominously. To the side of the duty desk was a double set of doors that led into the barracks. Arram knew the Officer of the Day's office was there, and likely that's where Major Jaekman was.

"Sit him down somewhere and let him cool his heels a while,

said the sergeant to the men now surrounding Arram. "He'll be glad to see the last of us after a good long sit, and won't soon be coming back."

"Should we call Major Jaekman?" asked one soldier who still held Arram by the elbow.

"Oh now you wish to waste more people's time," said the sergeant adding in a rather loud and imperious tone, "well, we will not be wasting Major Jaekman's valuable time."

"Who is planning to waste Major Jaekman's time?" called a voice from beyond the double doors and an officer of the Guard looking relaxed in a well-tailored semi-dress uniform, the jacket open and the collar undone, stepped out. Arram recognized Major Jaekman and knew he had just returned from a meeting at the palace.

The men of the watch snapped to attention, Arram's elbows were liberated with the precision of their response and the crispness of their salute. The duty sergeant, too, was at attention, his salute as crisp as the men of the Watch, The major returned their salute and said, "As you were, gentlemen," and turned toward the sergeant a questioning look on his face.

"Beggin' your Major's pardon, sir, said the flustered duty sergeant, "sorry for wastin' your time, sir. This elderly fellow was makin' smart and asking to see you, sir. I brought him in to cool his heels for a while before sending him off."

The sergeant turned to the members of the watch, "sit him down in Interview Room one, He said.

"One moment," said the Major, "let me look at this brave soul who seems to have disconcerted the Duty Sergeant and his watch and dared to ask for me by name."

He strode over to Arram scanning him up and down as he approached. He stopped a step from Arram and looked into his

132

eyes. He recognized this man, then realizing whom it was, he froze a moment.

"Colonel," he blurted, "Colonel Nevil!"

He stepped back, and for a brief moment, one could detect the beginnings of a salute. Jaekman caught himself, then half question half exclamation, "It is you, Colonel Nevil, isn't it?"

The four men of the Watch and their sergeant watched in confusion and discomfort. Something was happening here that was beyond their understanding.

"It is, indeed, Major," affirmed Arram, "and I must commend you on the excellence of your gateman and watch. Your sergeant, I can tell, is an old campaigner.

"Thank you, sir," said the Major, then he relaxed. "Colonel, where have you been? We have not heard from you in years. General Beckenham and, indeed, our beloved Majesty, himself, have been searching for you for all these years. Your sword and uniform still reside in your old locker, still awaiting your return. In fact, you, sir, have become quite a legend around here."

"But look at you, sir, dressed like a hawker, and a donkey cart… I'm presuming that is yours standing outside the gate. It must be as only a donkey trained by Colonel Arram Nevil would stand so calm and patient without a hobble or tie."

Turning towards the members of the Watch and a dismayed duty sergeant, Major Jaekmen, struggling to fight back the emotion that was threatening his words. He spoke in what he hoped was a casual tone, "Gentlemen of the watch, Duty Sergeant Striper, let me introduce you to someone whose name you've often heard around here, but a face you've never seen. This, gentlemen, is Colonel of the Royal Guard, member of the household guard, first bodyguard of the prince, now King Rafael, former chief of the Palace Watch and often decorated national hero, Colonel Arram Nevil."

All five, Watch and duty sergeant snapped to ramrod attention and were raising their hands in salute when Arram interrupted, "Please gentlemen, no salute, I am not in uniform, nor have I been for many years, but I will shake your hand if you allow me."

Allow they did, thrilled knowing they would have a great story to share back in their quarters tonight. They were the first to meet the famed Guard legend, Colonel Nevil. "Now, Colonel, what caused you to break your long silence and come to see me dressed in what appears to be hand-me-downs from a tinker?"

"Well, Alf, "returned Arram, "they aren't hand-me-downs, and you, I remember as an eager cadet who rode with me as an observer with the late king on a state visit to Durain. You impressed me then, and I have followed your progress through the ranks over the years. I have something important to tell, and I believe you are the one best prepared to deal with what I have to say. Can we talk privately?"

"Sir, follow me.

"Call me Arram, please," said Arram following Jaekman to one of the interview rooms. "No one has sirred me for many years and now it makes me feel uncomfortable."

Jaekman had guided Arram to one of the back interview rooms. After about twenty minutes, Jaekman, a concerned look on his face, threw open the door and called to the duty sergeant, "Sergeant," he shouted, "sound the bell."

Although startled, the sergeant ran to the large bell that hung on the wall beside the double doors and struck it with a metal gavel that hung beneath it. The bell, not been rung in years now echoed through the barracks.

A single strike of that bell would bring officers running to the reception area. At the same time, the regular guardsmen would be pulling on combat uniforms as they ran to their assigned arms lockers to gather their weapons and battle gear. They would then return to their bunks to await orders. Despite the fact the bell had never rung during their lives in the service, all in the barracks reacted with the precision and speed of well-trained soldiers.

Arram was confident that the guard under Jaekman would be on its way, well prepared to deal with those treasonous potential assassins of the monarch. Knowing he would only be a distraction, he slipped out the door, but not before the duty sergeant approached him to offer his apology for his abrupt behavior. "Think nothing of it, sergeant, "smiled Arram, "it's crusty sergeants like yourself that have made the Guards the efficient and skilled force it is."

The sergeant smiled, trying to conceal the puff of pride he felt from the famous Colonel Nevil's compliment. He turned back to await the upcoming briefing. He and the men of the watch stayed to secure the barracks. Jaekman would gather his elite mounted warriors and head north while the others would spread through the city maintaining a condition of high alert.

Passing through the gate, he gave the guard a smile, "Everything is well in hand, private, keep to your duty and don't worry about what's going on inside. It's being handled with the traditional precision of the Royal Guard."

Arram clambered onto the donkey cart, "Let's go Jezzie, We have some business to take care of."

He had an extensive knowledge of the city and its surroundings. This and his knowledge of the movements of royalty allowed Arram to get to the route the royal party would take, well ahead of them. He reined in Jezzie, and she began a slow and stately amble along the road, a pace that guaranteed to upset the protocol officer and bring Arram to his and the king's attention.

27

XXVII. Business and Pleasure

As the morning progressed, it found an uncomfortable Underlieutenant standing at the palace entrance dressed in his riding outfit. He was led into the dining hall where Her Majesty, Queen Alyssa, Prince Micha and Roisin stood around a chair in which sat a still pale, but much healthier Princess Emmaline. Matricht saluted and waited to be addressed. "Underlieutenant Matricht," said the Queen walking towards him, "please, relax. Would you like some coffee while we wait for His Majesty?"

She showed him to the table. Then, the queen, herself, poured coffee into a cup and handed it to him. "Do help yourself; I don't know how you prefer it."

"Your Highness," he returned, with a deferential bow.

"Please, Underlieutenant Matricht," said the Queen, "you are very important to us all. It was you who gave us back our daughter. We could never express how grateful we are to you. You are among friends."

At that moment, the king burst through the door, "Ah, good, you're here," he said to no one in particular.

Breakfast was informal as the Queen's message had promised. The Queen made every effort to put the Underlieutenant at ease, and he soon was. It surprised him to discover it was much like mealtime at his own family home. The conversation around the table was relaxed, and soon he joined in the talk.

By the time breakfast was over, he had chatted with the King about his father's military record; to the queen about his mother's prize roses, to Princess Emmaline about his home on the edge of the forest; to Micha about basic training and to Roisin about Palisade Market. He was so enjoying himself the time flew by. It seemed only moments after King Rafael had arrived that he was up and headed for the door calling to the Underlieutenant over his shoulder it was time they got about the day's business.

King Rafael led him to the royal stables. He presented several differ carriages of different sizes with a sweep of his hand. "Which should I take on this journey, Underlieutenant?"

"Well," returned Underlieutenant Matricht with some reluctance, "To tell you the truth, Your Majesty, the road is rather rough and narrow. You might find it a better trip on horseback."

"By Jove," said the King, "horseback! I like this, business and pleasure together."

A Short time later, the king, Prince Micha, Underlieutenant Matricht and a small retinue of courtiers, including a young protocol officer rode out through the western gates of the palace. Had the king sought anonymity, the protocol officer made certain it was not to be. At every intersection, he stopped traffic to let the king's party pass. Along the streets, he waved traffic to the curb and rushed pedestrians to the sidewalk with a loud, "Make way for the king."

When it was obvious, this was causing quite a stir among the populace, King Rafael called the young protocol officer over to him. Praising him for his fine work, he then suggested that he play down their presence and not to disrupt the citizens as they carried out their day's affairs.

By the time they arrived at the northern edge of the city, they were passing through the streets unnoticed. So unnoticed in fact, that the party ended up behind a donkey cart and was unable to pass. The protocol officer could contain himself no longer. He rode up beside the driver and berated him. The driver slowed his donkey and, ignoring the protocol officer, turned back towards the king and his party. "That's him," exclaimed Matricht, "He's the one who told me where I could find the girl."

"Then I owe him my thanks," said the king who rode up beside the now stopped cart and dismounted.

The old man climbed down from his cart and stood before his king. He bowed his head and then faced the king. King Rafael took one look into those steel grey eyes and to the amazement of the rest of the party, shouted, "Arram. It's Arram. I can't believe it. You're still alive," and he grabbed the old man in a fierce embrace

Holding the old man at arm's length, he turned to Matricht and the retinue. "This, gentlemen, is Colonel Arram Nevil, retired, of the Royal Life Guards. Why when I was Micha's age, I led him on many a merry chase."

"Aye, that you did, sire," responded Arram with a grin, no trace of the rustic in his voice, "but not near so much as the young Prince Micha will run the Underlieutenant, here."

"The Underlieutenant is, I believe, attached to Emmaline's retinue, Arram," explained the king.

Arram smiled and in a tone he had used more than once before with Rafael, said, "Your Majesty, the Princess' will always be of fragile health. Much of the time, she will remain close to home. Such a sedentary life would offer little challenge to this clever and resourceful young officer. It would be such a waste."

"Good point," said the king as he turned to face the protocol officer. "Have Colonel Habbiger reassign Matricht to the retinue of the Prince. In fact, you may tell him it is my wish he be Micha's personal bodyguard."

"Yes, Your Majesty..." the protocol officer's voice trailed off.

"Do you have difficulty with that," asked the king.

"Well, sir," responded the protocol officer carefully, "traditionally, a personal bodyguard must have met certain standards. For one thing, he must be a full officer. The Underlieutenant is... well... an Underlieutenant."

"Then have Habbiger grant him a full commission," said the king, his tone commanding, and he turned back to Arram.

"How was that?" asked the king.

"A most impressive display of regal authority, Your Majesty," said Arram with a laugh.

The king grinned, and then as if a cloud had passed, his expression changed. "But, what of you, Arram? What has brought you to this? You dress like the lowest and poorest of peasants. Why?"

Arram smiled, "Your Majesty, it is a long story, but this is not the time to tell it. You ride to the north, I believe."

"Yes, of course," replied the king remembering what had led to this encounter.

"This is a most momentous occasion, sire, you must be off."

"Momentous, I would..." the king did not continue his thought. He had known Arram too well and if Arram said it was momentous, then somehow, it was.

"How so?"

"Do you know how many centuries have gone by since a reigning monarch of Bantira has ridden in state to visit his most faithful cadet, the Grand Duke of the North Reaches?"

Puzzlement was the only response of the king.

Arram continued, "Yes, I'm afraid the monarchs have been neglectful of their subjects. You will find Duke Theodore much like me, wearing the attire of the lowest and poorest of peasants. In his poverty, he may have forgotten his heritage, but I have not."

"I know of no Duke of the Northern Marches. The line has long since died out."

No, sire, the line remains. Drought and desolation usurped it and years of hard work, and poverty caused it to be forgotten. The hard-working pauper, father of the girl you have as a guest in the palace, is the rightful heir to that title. Now, be on your way, Majesty, this is a special day for this great dominion. My story will wait."

As he mounted his horse, Rafael, in his most regal tone addressed the old man. "Know you, Arram, former colonel of the Royal Life Guards and bodyguard to the once crown prince and always, our dearest friend, before too many days have passed, by royal command, you will come before us in an audience and tell that story."

Arram bowed his head. "I await Your Majesty's command."

He steered his donkey Jezebel and cart to the side of the path and watched the king's party ride past. "It is, indeed, a most momentous day," he murmured to Jezebel as he scratched her behind one of her long floppy ears and pulled in behind the king's retinue. He closed his eyes for a second. The haunting image of the dappled mare and young rider balancing on the

141

edge of disaster was still there. This time, however, it seemed much farther away, as if seeing it through a reversed telescope.

Jezzie had no problem keeping up with the riders, and once they had made their way beyond the city streets and the crowds that gathered at every intersection to cheer their king as he passed, the pace picked up some. However, while this was new to the king and his retinue, it was familiar territory for Arram and his donkey. They had no difficulty navigating the narrowing trail and keeping in step with the riders.

While the Vanguard ranged ahead, Matricht and then Prince Micha followed just behind the king, his personal guard, and the young protocol officer. Arram followed just behind the rear guard.

XXVIII. More Surprises on the Road

As they approached the place where the riverbank curved left beside the slate hills, they met Major Jaekman and his men with a large group of prisoners in tow. The only one of the king's party not surprised by this was Arram. It was he, of course, who had informed Major Jaekman of the plot to ambush the king as he and his retinue rode unaware below the slate hills.

The impending attack had been foiled.

While the captain of the king's guard along with the king rode ahead to meet with Major Jaekman, from whom they would learn the details of the thwarted attack, Arram surveyed the collection of captured men and saw that two notable were missing.

Climbing down from his cart, Arram scanned the surrounding landscape from the slate hills to the banks of the riverbed where a muddy trickling stream and tall grasses vied for a place in the wide, sandy bed. As Arram moved closer to the river bank for a clearer look at the thicket below, one of Major Jaekman's men approached him carrying a belt and scabbard bearing a military saber. "Major Jaekman told me to give you this," he stated in a curt and respectful military tone and proffered the belt and saber out to Arram.

Taking the offer, Arram thanked the soldier and belted it on. He drew the saber and saw it was as sharp and clean as on the day he had left it. It drew easily from the well-oiled scabbard.

The saber felt very comfortable in Arram's grip. It was as if no time had passed since he had last drawn it to place it at the feet of his king and commander-in-chief.

In years past Arram had worked so hard to develop his sword handling skills with this very sword, and he could sense that even after so many years away, that his hand still kept the fluid grace of the master swordsman.

"Ah, Arram, Your sword," said the king as he approached him on his way back to his mount. "How I've missed it. Remember how we would take turns playing share the apple? Thanks to you and it, I am no slouch at fencing... but a saber," he said to no one in particular, "Ah, a saber." And his voice drifted off.

"Excuse me a moment, sire," said Arram, "there is something I must do."

As he spoke, he moved toward the riverbank, was over the side and gone from sight before Rafael could comment or ask what it was he must do.

XXIX. Vengeance at Last

A swampy odor engulfed Arram as he descended into the riverbed. He could see where the muddy stream had become several tinier trickles some of which ended in small, scummy puddles.

He could see faint traces of footsteps although they were barely detectable as someone had attempted to brush them away. Not surprisingly, those faint footprints headed towards a nearby grove of reeds and cattails.

Examining the grove, Arram had to admire the careful effort it must have taken to conceal the passage of two men through the ragged growth. He knew it was not the handy work of the haughty and impetuous Leonis. This was that of the canny ex-Ranger, Arve. Before the Rangers were disbanded, they were little more than a ceremonial group only used for state parades and coronation honor guards. By the time Arve joined the already depleted ranks, the remaining Rangers' duties would have been light, but this former elite fighting force had never relaxed its extreme training protocols.

As Arram moved deeper into the grove following the minimal

hints of passage, he heard stealthy breathing. This was someone, as Arram could easily determine, who was untrained in strict concealment. He knew he would never hear the slightest sound coming from a trained Ranger.

"Why, your highness," he called out as he turned and moved toward the hidden Duke, "playing at Seek and Hide? Somewhat indecorous for someone of your position, don't you think?"

As he had hoped, the Duke would bolt on being discovered which would allow Arram to focus on the more dangerous Arve.

Arram had cut around the hiding Duke so that in bolting he would head for that portion of the riverbank where the King with his guard and Jaekman with his troops waited. At that very moment, he sensed movement and stepped out of the grove with just enough time to see Arve; sword raised for a killing stroke rush towards him.

He parried Arve's overhand deathblow with his sword, and took a braced stance, facing the former Ranger. The fight was short but furious with Arve slashing and striking out while Arram worked to parry and ward off each intended blow. While Arve was fighting to wound, or kill Arram with strokes to the body core, Arram was looking for his opening, and when he found it, his defense became a lightning attack. Arram was not looking for the killing stroke but went for Arve's left leg. In a move reminiscent of the game, he had played with the then Prince Rafael that they called "Share the Apple," Arram turned his blade sideways and swung it at the leg severing muscle and tendon just behind Arve's knee.

With a look of surprise, Arve dropped to the ground. A second stroke from Arram's sword disarmed him as he fell. "Ah, don't fret, Arve," said Arram, "you'll walk again, but maybe not as fast."

Arram turned and raced after Leonis who, in his terror was trying to scale the sandy riverbank. Arram, leaping from tuft of grass to tuft of grass, better anchored than the bare sand, ascended the hill and passed the scrambling Duke. At the top of the bank, he knelt and held out his hand to Leonis. He grabbed the panicking Duke by the wrist and dragged him up the bank.

Leonis, looking up and seeing Arram's face had his momentary relief turn to surprise and fear. He recognized the face of Colonel Nevil. "Aye, "Said Arram, "rather than pulling you up, I could have left you. No one would question a wound to the Grand Duke's jugular. One should never climb a slippery slope with a dagger in one's hand."

"And so," he continued, "I give to you something you never gave to my niece, your life."

Arram turned away from the speechless Leonis and made his way to the gathered members of the king's guard and Jaekman's troop. "Here," he called, "is the perpetrator of this adventure and below, near the scrub you'll find Arve, former captain of the Rangers. He is inconvenienced by a leg wound and should be no trouble to gather up."

He walked over to the now informed King Rafael astride his horse. "I believe, Majesty, that it is time to continue this very important journey."

"God forgive me, Arram," replied the King, "I never knew, I never knew. Leonis was the ruffian who killed your niece. We must make right!"

"Duke Theodore is more important now than Duke Leonis, Sire," said Arram," and Jaekman will take good care of him.

He turned to his courtiers and guards, "Gentlemen," he said, "enough of this diversion. Let us be on our way and oh," he said pausing a moment, "would someone let Colonel Nevil borrow his horse so he can ride at my side?"

"I will," shouted Matricht.

He dismounted and walked over to Arram holding out the reins, "uncle," was all he said.

"My thanks, nephew," returned Arram. And you may ride on Jezzie's cart. I'm sure she'll take to you, after all, you are family."

And so, the royal trek into the North Reaches continued.

30

XXX. Duke of the North

The rest of the journey was uneventful except for the shocking scenes of desolation the Royal party encountered along the dry bed of the once great Grande River.

The servile greeting Rafael received from Roisin's family startled him. How could these people, steeped in hardship and desperation be loyal to a king who had so neglected them?

Dismounting, he walked to Ned and his wife and with his hands raised them from their knees to stand face to face with him. "I come to you, not as a sovereign, but as a father who owes you and your daughter much. I am, like yourself, sir, a father who only wishes to express his undying gratitude and ask you to come back with us to the palace and join your daughter whom you must be missing. As one father to another, I ask you to please come with us so we may honor you and show our gratefulness."

Pointing to Arram, he added, "And, if Colonel Nevil is correct, and knowing his honesty, wisdom, and loyalty, which I do, you are, in fact, the Grand Duke of this dry and desolate land.

That means you are ever free to stand before me as a peer and member of the nation's council of state."

Stepping in front of his father, Micha offered, "So will you come? Rosie wants to see you."

A bewildered Ned turned to his wife who nodded yes.

Rafael hesitated, "Well I guess you will need to take care of things before we go. Do you have someone to watch the house, or should I leave some of my Guard?"

Ned shook his head, "my oldest son and his young wife will look after it. As for my wife and I, we have little, but let us at least don our festival clothes as our workaday clothing shows little honor to you."

"Fiddle, faddle, "said the king, "but do as you wish. We will wait here until you are ready."

31

XXXI. A New Balance

Before the day was through, Ned and his family had joined Roisin in the palace. Ned was no less surprised than the King had been earlier to learn he was the direct heir of the Grand Duke of the North Reaches and First Guardian of the Great River Crossing. There was no disputing it, the Royal Genealogist had the proof and the court historian, and archivist confirmed it.

To be sure, nothing was grand about the North Reaches, nor was there any great river to cross. Still, Ned, now, much to his consternation, Theodore, was to have a formal introduction to the court as Grand Duke of the North.

Underlieutenant Matricht was greeted on his return to the palace with a full commission and put into the service of Prince Micha much to the young Prince's delight. Pleased as he was by all this, the newly minted Captain Matricht could not help remembering his first encounter with the youthful prince and the thoughts he had back then reechoed in his mind: "His bodyguard will have his hands full.

Princess Emmaline's health was restored and Lady Roisin

installed as a Lady in Waiting in her retinue, Prince Micha decided the three companions were ready to resume their adventures. So they did, giving Captain Matricht a taste of what was to come. Prince Micha fulfilled old Arram's predictions and more. It was a merry chase.

32

XXXII. Retribution

To say King Rafael was devastated by the conditions he encountered in the northern part of his domain was an understatement. He was a kind man who cared for his family and his subjects. To discover that so many of his subjects lived with such hardship troubled him and he pledged that he would do all in his power to improve their lot. The bleak facade of the North Tower, which had so long concealed the desolation of the North, became the daily reminder of its unhappy presence.

The Grand Duke and his men were in exile in the Complines, an archipelago of small islands and salt marshes in the distant South Sea. "There," the king had stated, "Leonis can recreate his Grand Duchy for the scallops and the marsh puppies."

"But don't count him out, "Arram told Rafael, "I believe he will do everything in his power to return and seek revenge."

"Indeed," The King made a dismissive wave "In the meantime, would you hold the West March for me, as Lord Nevil, Arram?"

"You do me honor, your majesty," said Arram, "And you may burden me with titles and as your loyal subject I will accept, as long as no one speaks them too loudly. I believe Sir Stanley would make an excellent supervisor of the province of West March and its castle. I would like to join Ned O'Reaches and see what we can do to restore that land to its former bounty. Perhaps we might even get that river flowing again."

"Well, "said the king, "if there's one thing I know for certain, when your mind is set, Arram, you are not easy to dissuade, so restoring the North Reaches it is. "

"Well, then get to it, Lord Nevil, "said the king as he turned to wink at his daughter, the princess and her dearest friend, Lady Roisin.

Captain Matricht and Prince Micha were already off on some adventure.

With the North Tower as a constant reminder of the neediest of his subjects, King Rafael was ever mindful of doing whatever he could to assist the residents of the North Reaches. Despite all this, life would still be hard for those in the North, until the great river once again flowed through the land. But that would be another story.